BROKEN LIKE GLASS

BREE LIVINGSTON

Edited by
CHRISTINA SCHRUNK

Bree Livingston
Publishing

Broken Like Glass / Bree Livingston. -- 1st ed.

ISBN: 9798633459326

To the broken.

To my readers,

This is not my usual book. In fact, it is not like any of my other books. For starters, it's written in first person present.

It is not a romance, although there is some romance in it. It is not a mystery, although there is some mystery in it.

To be honest, I'm not sure what category it fits in. I can tell you two things about it.

First, it is not light reading. It is not something to read if you are looking for something fluffy as an escape from day to day life. There are lots of books for that, including my other books, but this is something completely different.

Second, it has a significant amount of religious content. If that sort of thing offends you, then please check out my other books. I have plenty to choose from.

Although it is written by a woman, about a woman and for women, I think it can be read by anyone. I hope you do read it and I hope you enjoy it but, let me say it again. This is nothing like my other books, so please don't read this expecting the usual, because it's not.

-Bree

CHAPTER ONE

"Lillian. Lillian? Can you hear me, Lillian?" My therapist's voice grates on me. I'd say like nails on a chalkboard, but that wouldn't accurately describe just how much I hate her voice.

One flashy signature and a court order later, I'm sitting in this office for my first session, wishing I could be anywhere but here, especially since I've known her since we were kids.

She pelts me with question after question about my feelings.

"How did it make you feel, Ms. James?"

How did it make me feel? *How did it make me feel?*

I push out of the chair and walk to the window, wishing I could go back in time and never step foot in this town. I roll my eyes and then focus on the looming dark clouds that swirl as far as I can see.

Chrissy starts in again. "Lillian, the point of court-ordered therapy is to talk about what happened."

I close my eyes and concentrate on my breathing. In, out. In, out. In, out.

"Lillian, we really need to discuss what happened on Saturday. It's the only way you can heal."

In, out. In, out. In, out. *Dear God, please get me out of here.*

"Lillian," she says again, tapping her pencil against the clipboard she's holding like I'm wasting her time.

I bite my lip, count to ten, and turn

around. Leveling my gaze at her, I try to remain civil when I speak. "I don't want to talk about it. I don't want to heal right now. I don't want anything to do with any of this, and if it weren't for the fact that a judge forced me to be here, I'd be three hundred miles away in Austin by now."

"That may be, but you are here, and I have to report back to the judge on your progress. Help me understand why you stabbed your dad with a knife in the middle of the grocery store and then went home and smashed everything."

Another question I can't and don't want to answer. "Some people deserve a little knifing every once in a while, and his furniture was a hundred years past vintage. I'd say I did him a favor."

Chrissy purses her lips and looks at me with sympathy, which only intensifies my hatred of her.

"Lillian, everyone in this town knows

your father. The only reason you aren't facing jail time at the moment is because he wouldn't press charges and because the judge's wife babysat you as a child."

"The only reason I'm not in jail right now is because my best friend is an excellent lawyer." I lean back against the window. Rain is coming down hard enough now that I can feel it as it hits the glass.

"Well, again, I'm here to understand why you did it. If you don't cooperate, you may still be looking at jail time."

Pushing off the window, I walk to the chair facing her and flop down. "Maybe jail time would be good for me." This time, I don't meet her eyes. All my vim and vigor melted as I moved.

Chrissy looks at her watch. "Our time is almost up, but next time we meet, I expect you to actually talk. Do you understand?"

"Chrissy..."

"It's Dr. Blakely when you're here

during my business hours."

I lick my lips and try to control the desire to bolt from the room. "Dr. Blakely, I've known you since kindergarten. Don't you think it's a conflict of interest for you to be my therapist?"

"Lilly, come on. It's been fifteen years since we graduated from high school. Plus, I'm the only therapist in this little town. If you had waited to stab your dad in a bigger city, you could have had your pick of therapists."

"Some therapist you are."

"I'm an excellent therapist."

My heart drops in my stomach. I can't talk about what happened. I don't want to talk about what happened, and I definitely don't want to talk about what happened with Christine Blakely. "I don't even live here anymore. Surely Judge Kringle can find someone in Austin for me to see. They can report just as well there."

"You know he won't do that. He likes to keep things in town. He's old school. You're here for the next six months or until I tell him you are released."

"So, tell him I'm good."

Chrissy tilts her head and looks at me. "Lilly, I'm good, but I'm not that good. I'm not getting in trouble with Judge Kringle."

My shoulders sag, and I lean my head back against the chair.

"Why did you do it, Lilly? I've known your dad since I was just a little bitty. He's the nicest man I've ever known."

That's not true, and most of the people in this town know it's not. It's just polite to say one thing and think another.

I lift my head and level my gaze at her, keeping my expression unreadable. Words begin to float in my mind.

Chrissy looks down at her watch, and before I can give her a nasty answer, she tells me time is up.

CHAPTER TWO

When I came home to visit, I had no intention of making it more than a weekend trip. Instead, something inside me snapped, and now I'm stuck in Foaming Springs, Texas, until my court-ordered therapy runs its course.

As I walk down the sidewalk, people stare at me. Some even point. One of the drawbacks of growing up in a small town is that everyone knows you, your family, your family's history, your shortcomings, your everything, because what are people in a small town to do other than gossip? I jam my hands in my pockets and hang my head, trying to keep my face from being seen.

Exactly one hundred twenty-four paces from Dr. Blakely's private practice is the local bar, Kettlefish. It's the only bar and the closest to happy I'm going to get for a while. In my mind, I count the steps without looking up.

Sixty-eight more to go.

I can do this. I can walk these sidewalks, my head hanging down and hands in my pockets, and pretend I'm not here. The next six months will be a—

"Hey!"

Crud.

I look up, and there, in all his studly glory, stands Uriah Pendleton. "Lilly James?"

As if he doesn't know it's me. Yeah, it's

me. You know, the awkward nerd-chick who had the biggest, most embarrassing crush on you in high school? The one who asked you to the homecoming dance with a large banner, only to be told you'd already said yes to Misty Morning.

Yes, her parents named her Misty Morning. If she'd been ugly, the girl would have never made it through high school. As it turns out, the heavens shined down on her, making her the most popular girl in school. Lucky her. Not so lucky me.

"Yeah, it's me. Sorry for bumping into you."

He narrows his eyes. "Wait, did I hear something about you stabbing your dad?"

"Nope, got an evil twin. Gotta go now." I start to go around him, and he grabs my arm to keep me from walking. Uriah is still as good-looking as he was in high school, only his dirty-blond hair is cut short. He's just tall enough that I have to look up, and his face could melt the heart of a female Terminator.

His lips curve up, and his eyes sparkle. "I haven't seen you in town in ages. Just got back. We should get together sometime and catch up."

As if the flapping gums haven't reached him yet. Why on earth would he want to eat with me? "Well, in case you haven't been filled in yet, my schedule recently got a little more crowded, so it might take some real shuffling to find the time."

Uriah laughs, and it's like hot caramel. If only I were popcorn. Maybe if I'd seen him before going to the grocery store with my daddy, I'd have been less likely to stab the man who raised me.

"You're still funny, Lillian James. How about dinner tonight? I just got out of the Army, and I could use a few laughs."

What I really want to do is tell this

heartthrob to go make someone else gooey, but that face. I huff. "All right. I'd ask where, but there's, what, two places? Fried fish or fish fried?"

"Oh, no, there are three places now. You've been gone a long time. How about Tish's Tacos?"

"Tish opened a taco place?" I frown, thinking about Tish.

"People change, Lilly, people change."

"Fine. Tish's Tacos, but if I smell fish, I'm out."

Uriah laughs that silky laugh and flashes his heartbreaker smile. "See ya tonight, six sharp."

So, to recap my time so far, I've stabbed my daddy, turned my weekend into a six-month stay, and now I've got a something at six sharp with my high school crush.

I look at the sky. *You know, Papa, I'm ta-done with my ta-do list.*

I finish the sixty-eight steps to Kettlefish, push on the door, and stand face to face with my high school nemesis, Misty Morning.

CHAPTER THREE

"Well, looky here. It's Lillian Loser James," Misty drawls out loud enough that everyone in the bar turns my direction.

"Hello, Misty," I say and try to walk around her.

She sidesteps with me and keeps me from walking farther into the bar. "You sure you should be drinkin'?"

I take a deep breath. Six months, Lilly, just six months, and Foaming Springs will be nothing more than a bad dream. Instead of saying anything, I try to sidestep again, and, of course, the she-beast stops me again.

"I think we'd all like an answer. What with your propensity to stab people."

"Propensity? That's a mighty big word, Misty. Did you look it up as you saw me walk in the bar?"

Her lips curl, and she raises an eyebrow. "I went to college."

Just as my brain is revving out of neutral and into first gear, Fancy Coleman speaks up. "Misty, ain't you got somewhere else to get wet? Leave Lilly alone or get."

Misty throws an exasperated look over her shoulder and smiles. Like she's the one who's been insulted. "See ya later, Lillian." Her voice drips a noxious potion some-where between poison and sunflowers.

"Hey, girl." Fancy walks around the bar and envelops me in a bear hug. "How's my favorite nerd?"

I shrug my shoulders and let her walk me to the bar. She pushes me onto a stool and walks behind the counter where she slides a glass in front of me and fills it with a clear liquid. "Here, demons ain't got no chance with that."

"Water?"

"Rum."

I pick up the glass and throw the drink back. It burns going down my throat, but for the first time since I arrived in town, my nerves seem to settle. "Smooth," I choke out.

"Don't need smooth, just gone." Fancy smiles and pours more in my glass. She folds her arms and leans down on the bar. "Honey, you got people talkin'."

I grunt a laugh. "They were talkin' long before I got here."

She points her finger at me, and her eyebrows lift to her hairline. "Yeah, but now they talkin' 'bout you."

"What's new?" I ask with a shrug. Not like these people didn't run their mouths before I left town. They all knew my family. Knew my daddy and how terrible he could be. It just wasn't polite to speak of it.

"Sweetie, you always could find trouble."

"I find trouble? Me? I fix computers. I like *Star Wars*, *Doctor Who*, and *Firefly*. Trouble seems to find me even when I'm hiding under a sofa." My voice has gone from a hushed whisper to high-pitched without me realizing it. I look around, and the people staring at me turn away.

"Well, I guess you came out from under the sofa this time, huh? What'd you go and do that for anyway?" Fancy clamps a hand down on my arm.

I swallow hard. I didn't have an answer for Chrissy, and I sure don't have one for Fancy. Even if I did, I don't think I'd want to tell it here. "I'd need a long couch, six valiums, and more rum for that."

Fancy lets my arm go and stands up with her arms crossed over her chest. "You need to figure it out, then, before it comes out uglier than you can shake a stick at." She locks her eyes with mine, and I can tell she's about to be serious with me. "Lilly, get to church, find Jesus, or whatever you need to do, but whatever's going on in that head of yours needs to be out. Keeping that kinda stuff in can make a person lose themselves."

I keep my eyes pinned on the liquid in the glass. If the words were so easy to get out, then maybe I wouldn't have shanked my daddy or destroyed his house. Whatever was inside me just kinda crawled out, wiggling like a worm on a rainy day, and now it was stuck on the pavement, waiting for a bird to pick it off.

Fancy pats my arm when I kept quiet. "Okay, I'll just leave this here." She sits the bottle in front of me. "I'll be here if you need me." Then she saunters off to the end of the bar to talk to Marlin, the oldest coot in town. Not my words, his.

A shiver shimmies down my spine, and I fix my gaze on my glass again. I hold the glass with two hands and slide it around on the bar in a circular motion, the rum never quite getting high enough to spill over the edges.

When I stop long enough to really think, my heart hurts, physically. Why *did* I stab my daddy? I can't answer anyone because I don't know the answer.

We were in the grocery store, standing in the aisle with the pots and pans and other overpriced kitchen crud, and the next thing I knew, I was standing over him, holding a knife. He was holding his bloody shoulder, and people were yelling and screaming. It was just so fast, like I got body snatched or something.

A familiar person slides onto the stool next to me. I throw back my second drink and stare into the empty glass.

"So, now you drink, too?" My best bud and lawyer, Bo Anderson, reaches over the bar top and grabs a glass. Being the preacher's son, the only reason he can get away with being in the bar is that Fancy is a notary public. Of course, he could go to the courthouse, but the woman there is as mean as a snake to anyone without a head full of gray hair.

"Guess so. I've got a list of things to do before my six months is up."

"You need to slow down, then. This town gets mighty boring when the to-do list is finished." He laughs and pours himself a drink of water.

I rake a hand through my hair and rest my head in my palm as I look at him. "I thought you had some court thing today?"

As the only lawyer in a small town, court days are few and far between—unless, of course, old friends show up, spilling blood in aisle six.

With a shrug, he lays his arms on the bar top and leans forward. "I postponed it. The Blakelys' crops are getting beat up with all of the hail lately, and they asked for my help to get it out of the fields before the next storms come through."

It's been a long time since I've thought about crops and hail. "I forgot about that."

"Yeah." He takes a drink and grunts. "You big-city folks tend to forget about that kind of stuff."

Turning to him, I scoff. "Big-city folk? I live in Austin. It's a six-hour drive."

"When a small town is in the rearview, it doesn't take long to forget the little people."

"Bo, what do you want? Did you come here to aggravate me?"

He laughs. It isn't like Uriah's. Bo has a

squishy laugh—not a bad laugh, but I like my popcorn covered in caramel, not soggy. Plus, Bo and I did that dance right before high school got out. It turned into two left feet the moment his lips hit mine. He looked at me, I looked at him, and it was over. Although, sometimes I think he was a little less certain than me, but I never did anything that might make him think there could be something.

I push my glass away and stand. "I'm going back to the hotel and packing my stuff. I'm renting that old cabin down by the woods."

"Mrs. Thompson's place?" he asks, surprised.

Nodding, I stuff my hands in my pockets. "Yeah, she's visiting family out West, and her daughter said I could rent it while I'm here."

"Need a ride?"

"Nah, I'll walk."

With a mock salute, he says, "See ya, Lills."

"Much later, Bo," I reply with the same thing we said to each other when we were kids.

CHAPTER FOUR

I leave Kettlefish and walk to the hotel I've been staying at. After my little culinary display at the grocery store and subsequent furniture destruction, I was arrested and then released on "personal recognizance" after a couple days. My first chore when I got out was to visit my old house and pack before Daddy got released from the hospital. The last thing in this world I want right now is to be face to face with him again.

My feet know which way to go, so my

brain plays on autopilot. Hands in my pockets, head down, doing my best to be as invisible as possible. So far, I'm batting zero and hoping my average is looking up—but, of course, I run into Jenny Walman.

Crud.

I look up at the sky again. *Really, Papa?*

"Hi, Lillian!" she says so brightly I think she bleeds neon. "How are you doing?"

"I'm…" I say and scratch my head. What am I supposed to say? I suck it up and spit out, "Okay." Okay?

"Well, I know things aren't great right now, but the church is hosting a Wednesday potluck tomorrow night if you want to come. I'm sure Pastor Jeffrey would love to see you. I know you and his son, Bo, were really good friends in high school." She talks like she's forty years older than me.

"We're the same age, Jenny."

She bats my arm and laughs. "I know that, silly."

"I've gotta get going, so…"

Jenny bounces on the balls of her feet and claps her hands. "Just say you'll come, okay? It'll be fun. Like when we were in high school. You, me, Bo, Uriah, Jimmy, Misty, and the whole gang from youth group."

I'm standing right here, God, just go ahead and kill me.

Instead of saying it out loud like I'd like to, I politely smile. "Okay, I'll be there. Is church still at six?"

"If it weren't for the potluck, it would be, but it's gonna be at five. Okay?" Jenny grins so wide her wisdom teeth peek at me.

"Five? I'll see you then."

She waves and continues down the street.

Now I've got dinner with Uriah tonight and a potluck tomorrow. Whoo. One hundred eighty-two days on the wall, take one down, pass it around, one hundred eighty-one days on the wall. I start to hang my head again and stop. Maybe if I look straight ahead, my luck will turn around.

I continue to the hotel and pass by the front desk to my first-floor room. The hotel smells like dirt, cotton, and chlorine. The indoor pool must be so clean it squeaks. My eyes burn a little, and I blink a few times as I push my key into the door-knob. Inside the room, I mill around, gathering up my things and stuffing them into my two suitcases.

Once my belongings are packed, I look around the room. I know myself well enough to know I need to go. Now. So, I snag the handles on my bags, pull the door open, and briskly walk to the front desk where I slap the key down.

Some woman I've never met comes waddling out of the back room and gives me a smile. The lipstick she's wearing must taste pretty good because it's smeared all over her front teeth. "Is that all, honey?"

"Yep, just put it on the card."

"Okay, sweets," she says.

The cabin I'm renting isn't all that far from the hotel. The sky has clouded over again, and I look down at my watch. I've got five hours before I'm supposed to meet Uriah. That's plenty of time to walk to the cabin, unpack, and scream into the void until my voice is hoarse.

My only wish is that the road was paved the whole way to the cabin. Dragging two suitcases with tiny wheels on wet dirt is a workout I wasn't planning on. If there was a decent place to buy clothes in town, I'd have tossed the suitcases and taken my chances. I also begin to wish my car wasn't impounded.

After pulling and tugging for what seems like forever, I finally get to the cabin and then tug and pull some more as I climb the steps. At least this place isn't making my eyes burn. It still smells like cotton and dirt, though.

Mrs. Thompson's daughter left the cabin unlocked and the keys lying on the counter in the kitchen. I stand in the doorway, looking the place over. "Home sweet home," I say aloud.

I can see a bedroom from the door and trudge over to it. When I asked about the place, I hadn't even bothered to check to see how many rooms. Why should I care? I'm a party of one. As long as it has a bed and indoor plumbing, I don't care.

Come to find out, it has two bedrooms. Maybe I'll make friends while I'm here. I bust out laughing.

I spend the next couple of hours putting my things away. No point in living out of a suitcase if I'm going to be here a while. When I'm done, I walk out onto the back deck. The woods butt up to the house, and all I can see for miles are trees. I can hear a stream somewhere too.

The railing is a bit rickety, but when I shake it, it seems to hold. I turn around, lean back on it, and take a deep breath. The rain has made everything damp, and it feels clean out here. As I stand there, I can feel claws working on my insides.

I hurt.

I hurt like the devil.

I love my daddy, and the last time I saw him, he was a bloody mess on the floor.

The sob that escapes my mouth shocks me to the core, and my knees hit the deck. My hand slides from the rail, and I'm lying in a ball, wrecked.

This town.

My daddy.

Memories hide in the shadows of my mind, trying to claw their way out.

How is Papa supposed to set me free

when I don't even know what I need to be freed from?

My chest hurts, and the water on the deck is soaking through my jeans and t-shirt. It's April, and chilly. I force myself up, and my shoes scrape the creaky wooden floor as I walk to the bathroom for a hot shower. As I strip off my clothes, I turn the knob and make sure the water's set to extra boiling.

The water rolls down my face, and I turn my back to it, letting it cascade down my spine. Any other time, I'd be screaming because of the temperature, but right now, at this moment, any cooler and it would be too cold.

I know it's coming time to meet Uriah, but I can't pull myself from the water until the hot runs cold. When I finally get out, I rub the fog off the mirror and look at myself. My eyes don't look too puffy, but I can see the redness in them. Maybe it'll be gone before I meet Uriah, or maybe he just won't see it.

CHAPTER FIVE

My walk back into town to Tish's Tacos is a lot less adventurous than my earlier walk. I guess whatever gossip was being spread has been applied liberally enough that they don't need to delve into hushed whispers as I walk through town anymore.

The smell hits me in the face as I walk in the door, and my stomach growls like a dragon guarding its nest. Uriah has already gotten us a table, and he waves me down. I sheepishly wave back as I walk to the table.

His grin is big and toothy and perfect. Just like in high school. "Hey, Uriah," I manage to croak out.

"Hey, Lills. I got you a soda. Is that okay?"

"That's good." I take a long drag on the straw, and the bubbles tickle my throat, making me cough.

Uriah laughs, and all I can think about is caramel and popcorn and gooey messes. He leans back in the seat, his big green eyes sparkling. My heart does a little dance. *Oh, God, have mercy on me.* This time, I'm earnestly praying.

"So," he says, "do I need to frisk ya, or you gonna behave?"

The question hits me like a dart, and I nearly drop my glass. "I've had my fill of body cavity searches. I'm on the straight and narrow from this point forward. I'm not looking for any trouble."

He leans forward on his arms and smiles

again. This time, the way he looks at me, I nearly choke on air. "Well, Lills, what are you looking for?"

"Uriah Pendleton. What is up with you? Don't you remember me asking you to the homecoming dance? You said no, remember?"

He chuckles and flashes me a wider grin, if that's possible. "I said no because I had already said yes to someone else. It was girl's choice, and I'd waited until the last possible moment for you to ask me."

I open and close my mouth a couple of times before my brain solidifies again. "You mean if I'd asked you sooner, you'd have actually said yes?"

"Lillian James, I've crushed on you since we were in the third grade. Don't tell me you didn't know. I know you did. I saw the way you batted your lashes at me and flirted."

"I didn't bat nothin'. Flirtin'? You mean

offering you something to drink when you were working in the churchyard or painting our house that one summer? Or hanging out during youth group?"

"Well, yeah."

"It was water. On a hot day. And youth group was…youth group. That's not flirtin'." That was just me…being me.

"Well, I did wait for you to ask me to the dance."

"I didn't know that." It seems like an understatement. All these years, and I had had no idea he waited or wanted me to ask him. I don't know how to process that.

Uriah looks at me like my pants are about to be engulfed in flames. "I told Misty and Jenny to tell you."

"Jenny would do what Misty told her to do, and Misty has hated me since before I was born. She's evil."

He throws his head back and laughs.

When he looks at me again, his smile touches every inch of my mind. "I've missed you so much, Lills. We used to hang out all the time when we were kids."

"In youth group." My voice raises an octave.

"Yeah, but we hung out. A lot. Youth group met at least once a week, and in the summer, we had stuff going on almost every weekend. You've always made me laugh. A girl with a mind is a beautiful thing."

Uriah Pendleton is sitting in Tish's Tacos, smiling at me and trying to put his caramel all over my popcorn. What in the world? Not that I don't like caramel, but I've spent the last fifteen-some years thinking I had a crush on him and it wasn't even close to mutual. Like he said, I'm a girl with a mind, and I feel like a jet just flew over my head.

"I had no idea," I barely whisper.

"Well, now you do."

My stomach growls again, and my cheeks warm.

"Let's get something to eat. You have any preferences?"

I shake my head because…words. Words seem to be far, far away.

He leaves the table, and when he returns, he's carrying enough tacos to feed an entire church. The food smells so good my mouth waters. "Here, let me get you another soda." He picks up my glass, smiles, and walks to the drink station.

I'm dazed. This must be a dream. When I planned my weekend at home, I was just coming back to see Daddy because I hadn't seen him since I left for college. Yeah, we'd kept in touch. By phone. He'd begged me to come home the last time I talked to him. I tried to say no, but the more I resisted, the more he begged. Finally, I just broke down and said I'd come to town.

When Uriah returns, he sets the glass in front of me and sits. "What are you thinking about, Lills?"

"Uh, nothing." I smile.

He narrows his eyes. "That didn't look like a nothing face."

I take a drink of my soda.

"Come on, talk to me. We used to be close."

"Past tense, Uriah. I've been gone a long time. I haven't talked to anyone in this town but Bo since I left after high school."

Uriah unwraps a taco and takes a giant bite. It gives my brain time to adjust, if that's possible. I realize when he stops chewing that it's not possible. I feel overwhelmingly unprepared for this moment.

"All right. Since we haven't talked in a while, tell me what's been going on with you," he says.

I take a deep breath and shrug as I open a taco. "Well, I went to a tiny little college down south after high school. Then I moved to Austin and worked for a computer software company for a while. About four years ago, I decided to start my own company."

Uriah's eyebrows shoot up. "Whoo. Look at you, Miss Thing. Owning your own company. Are they okay with you being here for a while?"

"I called my clients after it all happened. Told them kinda what was going on. Didn't really mention details, but they know I'll be here a while."

He smiles a smile that makes his eyes crease in the corners, and his lips look all kissable. I try not to stare, but it's really hard. Uriah Pendleton. *Oh, Papa, what are you doing?*

"So, just out of the military? Not reenlisting?" I ask.

Uriah shakes his head. "Nah, I've done fifteen. Five more and I could retire, but it's just not in me. Now that dad's passed away, I feel like I need to stay close to home."

"I heard about that. I'm sorry."

He shrugs, and I can see there's still sadness from the loss. I'm hurt for him, and at the same time, I'm glad that he had a daddy worth missing. "It's time I get out and try civilian life. I'd planned to come see you in Austin, but imagine my surprise when I ran into you today."

Again, I feel like I've been hit with a dart. "You were coming to see me?"

"Well, yeah, I've never stopped thinking about you. I'd ask Mom about you when I called, but she wouldn't have anything to tell. When I'd talk to Bo, he seemed kinda dodgy. So I figured the best way to find out what you've been up to was to come see you."

"Bo was dodgy?"

"Yeah, Bo was dodgy. I'd ask him questions, but he didn't like me asking about you."

I blink, trying to think why Bo would be like that. "Huh. I don't know why."

Uriah's eyebrows knit together as he's looking at me like I should know. "'Cause he's sweet on you. He's been sweet on you forever. For a smart girl, you sure don't know about men, do ya?"

I sigh. "Uriah, that is the understatement of the century."

He laughs again. Head back, throaty laugh. Uriah is still the same guy I knew in high school, only he's got big arms now, a buzz-cut growing out, and a confidence he didn't possess when I knew him back when. "Lills, I know you aren't here under great circumstances, but I'm glad I ran into you. You going to the potluck tomorrow night?"

Groaning, I roll my eyes. "Jenny roped me into going."

"What, you don't go to church anymore?"

I kinda wither under Uriah's intense gaze. Church isn't something I like anymore. I don't know when or why I stopped, but the thought of going tomorrow night makes me ache in ways I don't understand. "I stopped going a long time ago. You mean to tell me you still go?"

"Yeah, I go. Well, I don't just go. In the Army, I was a chaplain."

It's my night for surprises. "You?"

"Yeah, me. I'll pick you up tomorrow, okay?" He winks, and my heart stutters.

"Uriah, I can walk."

"I'm sure you can, but I'm picking you up."

"Are you sure you want to be seen with me? I mean, we both know how mouths run in this town."

"Let 'em run. I don't care." He winks at me again.

This trip home has turned out nothing like I expected, and I'm not sure what to think at this point.

CHAPTER SIX

Uriah's 80s Ford pickup rumbles and then dies as we sit in front of my rented cabin. After tacos, he insisted on driving me home. To tell the truth, I hadn't been all that excited to walk in the dark. It wasn't the two-legged bogeyman I worried about as much as the four-legged ones.

The walk had felt quick, even dragging my unwieldy suitcases, but the drive seemed like nothing. I sat quiet the whole way. What was I supposed to say? I feel like I've been clubbed over the head the entire day. Plus, something keeps chewing on my mind. Like there's a door with someone pounding on it, screaming to be let out, and I'm not ready.

We sit in the truck, and out of the corner of my eye, I can see Uriah staring at me. He sits with his back to the door and his leg up on the seat. I have no idea what he's expecting. What he wants me to say.

"Lills…" he starts to say, but I can hear a tone that makes me feel like I need to give him a warning.

"Something's wrong with me," I blurt, and then more words just fall out. "I don't know what it is or how to put it into words right now, but you need to know. I'm broken, and it's a kind of broken that glue can't fix."

Uriah takes a deep breath and touches my arms. "Lills. Lilly."

He wants me to look at him, but I just can't. I can't see those big sparkly green eyes in the dark, but I know they're there. If I look at him, I won't be able to keep my distance, and I need to.

"Lilly, look at me."

"No." I look out the window and focus on the shadows.

"Why can't you look at me?" The way his voice sounds, the tenderness in it, pricks at me.

I close my eyes and purse my lips, keeping my face away from him. If I cry in this truck, I'm not sure I'll be able to stop.

"Lills, I don't know what's going on with you, but I'm here." There's that caramel again. Just hot enough to stick on your fingers without burning them. "I know it's been a while, but there's something here. I feel it."

I peel my eyes from the shadows and look at him. The half-moon is hitting the paint on the hood of the truck, bouncing off and illuminating his face. My heart flutters. Even in the dark, Uriah is perhaps the best definition of good-looking I've ever known.

"I'm a good listener, you know? That's most of what an Army chaplain does. Listen."

"I don't have the words, Uriah. I don't have the words. I don't even know what it is I'd need the words for right now."

"But you'll talk to me when you find them, right?" He locks eyes with me. It's the same way as when we were kids. The way he had of making me feel like I was Goldilocks and he was the porridge that was just right.

"I don't know." I pull my eyes away from him and look down at my hands in my lap.

Quick as lightning, Uriah moves, and he's sitting right next to me with his arm around my shoulder. "Even if this goes nowhere, Lilly. Even if all we get out of it is being really good friends for the rest of our lives, I want you to know I'm here. According to the Army, I've got perfect hearing too."

Clearly, the Army doesn't have enough tests because his hearing isn't the only thing that's perfect. When I twist to look at him, his breath hits my cheek. Even with his taco breath, my insides feel like wax under a blowtorch.

He seems so open, so put together, so... Uriah, only more mature. I can't help but nod my head and say, "Okay."

Those big Army-conditioned arms envelop me in a hug so gentle that if I were a muffin, all my stuffin' would still be intact. His lips move against my hair. "Lilly, it's going to be okay. I don't know how, or when, or anything, but I know it's going to be okay."

Oh, Papa, please don't make me cry in this truck with Uriah holding me like this. The bad, horrible thing I've done will only be worse if I hurt him. What if you can't fix me? What if my kind of broken is the kind that jabs people and makes them bleed? I can't handle another clean-up on aisle six. Especially not Uriah Pendleton.

He doesn't let go for a long time, and for the first time in years, I feel like someone is pressing me together just hard enough that I might actually mend. It feels so good to be wanted and warm. I search my mind for a time when I've felt wanted, and there's nothing but a blank.

I know Momma and Daddy loved me, right? So why do I feel like this? If I've never felt wanted, how do I know what it feels like? Is this wanted or just something else I don't have a definition for?

Eventually, I stand on the stairs, holding a bag of extra tacos he's given me, watching him leave. The cold air works its way into my pores so deep I'm shivering by the time I walk in my door.

I stand in the dark living room, my

mind a whirl like those dark clouds earlier in the day. My breath comes out in puffs. Evidently, I didn't turn the heat on before I left, and in true Texas April form, it's freezing inside the cabin. A shiver runs down my spine into my toes, so I fumble in the dark for the light switch and flick it on.

It was bright enough earlier that I didn't need a light. Now, in the dark, I need light as only one bulb seems to be functioning. Tomorrow, I will walk into town and get more. I count at least six between the living room and kitchen as I walk to the thermostat and set it in the seventies. At this point, I care less about the gas bill and more about my impending venture as an icicle.

I stick the extra tacos in the fridge and then make my way to the bedroom, flicking the light off in the living room and hitting the switch in the bedroom. Make that ten bulbs. I dress for bed in the moonlight, thankful this cabin sits out of town in the woods because of the lack of curtains over the windows. The sliding glass doors are big, and the moonlight covers the whole room in a hazy light.

I stand at the doors for a moment, taking in the woods surrounding the place. If this were an ocean, the cabin would be my life preserver, I guess.

I know Uriah said I'm not alone. I hear the words blazing in my brain, but they don't stop the feeling.

CHAPTER SEVEN

The next morning, Papa decides it should be bright and sunny, with a side of loud birds.

Worst alarm clock ever.

Birds are fine, just not this early. Even if early is not all that early as I squint at the alarm clock and its red block numbers tell me it's nearly noon.

I stretch so long and hard that my toes peek out the end of my blanket. My shoulders, spine, and neck crack in a couple of spots. The bed is lumpy and uncomfortable, but I slept like a stone in a creek. How, I'll never know other than maybe my body and mind were so tired that a bed made of needles would have worked just as well.

For a moment, I roll on my side and pull the covers up over my head with my eyes peeking out, looking through the glass doors. The birds are still loud, but I'm less cranky, so they don't bother me as much. That is, until a woodpecker decides to drill into a tree right outside the window. I take my cue from Woody and throw the covers off and hang my legs over the side of the bed.

My stomach gurgles and groans, and I frown. My list of to-dos didn't include grocery shopping yesterday. If I recall correctly, when I was putting up my stuff, I filled a drawer with some fruit bars. The thought propels me off the bed and in the direction of the kitchen.

On the way to the fruit-bar-filled

drawer, I stop by the thermostat and dial it down a notch. Life in Texas. One moment you're freezing to death, the next minute you're considering stripping.

I find the drawer full of bars, rip one open, and read the package: *A Slice of Heaven in Your Mouth*. Heaven is not what I experience when I bite into it. I rake the bite off my tongue with my finger and look at the rest of the bar. Tasting moldy armpit had not been on my bucket list, but at least now I can check it off.

Then I remember the bag of tacos Uriah handed me before I got out of the truck last night. "Thanks, Tish," I say and pull the handle of the fridge. The tacos are cold, but the aroma makes my stomach grumble even louder.

I snag the bag and pull a chair out to the deck. The legs squeak and bump on the wood floor as I drag it behind me. With my feet on the railing and my backside in the chair, I unwrap a taco and take a greedy bite. Cold or not, the taco tastes great, and if I compare it to the armpit fruit bar, it's downright delicious.

Birds flit and flirt in the canopy of the trees. Woody's still pounding away on the pine tree, his red head bright against the trunk of the tree. He stops for a moment and points his little beak at me like he's trying to decide if my head might be a good place to drill. I guess he decides against it because he starts back on the tree.

"You're a loud little sucker, ain'tcha?" I say to him.

In answer, Woody just hammers down.

As I unwrap my second taco, I fling the crumbs of the first one onto the deck, away from me. Maybe I can make friends with the birds. I bite into the second taco with the realization that I'm not as hungry as I was, and cold tacos aren't nearly as delicious the second time around. I almost wrap it back up, but I've come this far, so why not finish it? By the time I'm done, I'm wishing I hadn't been so persistent.

A light tap at the door breaks my attention from the birds I'm watching. I look over my shoulder, and Bo is standing at the door. I can see him through one of the glass panels framing the door. "Come on in," I yell and look back at the birds.

He stops on his way to the deck and grabs a chair, picking it up instead of dragging it. The legs land with a thud when he sets it down. "Good morning, good-looking. How are you today?"

I cut my eyes to him. "What?"

"You feeling any better?"

I shrug. "I don't know." It sounds harsh.

"Don't go biting my head off, Ms. James."

"Sorry, it came out worse than I planned."

The bag of tacos sits next to the leg of

my chair, and Bo reaches down and digs one out. "Tacos for lunch?"

"Breakfast. I just woke up."

"Any good?"

"Are you hungry?"

"Starved."

"Then they're delicious."

Bo eyes the taco warily.

"I've got some fruit bars you could sue for false advertisement." I hook a thumb in the direction of the kitchen.

"I'll stick with the taco." Bo unwraps it and picks off the wilted lettuce.

"Huh, I didn't even think to do that."

"Can't stand lettuce, and wilted lettuce is even worse."

Of course, I knew that. I've known Bo since forever, and lettuce might as well be a machete-wielding chupacabra. "You know, it's not evil."

"Says you." He finishes picking off the lettuce and inspects it for any lingering tiny green monsters. When he's satisfied the lettuce is gone, he takes a bite and chews loudly. "Good stuff," he says with his mouth full.

"Told ya."

Bo pauses eating a moment. "I think I may have persuaded Judge Kringle to let your car go."

That news should excite me, but I kinda like being chauffeured by Uriah. "Yeah?" I wiggle my toes as a breeze blows by.

The taco wrapper buzzes, and Bo grabs it so it doesn't fly off. "Yeah, but it would be more convincing if Chrissy backed me up. She said you didn't talk at all in therapy."

"It's Chrissy, Bo. I've known her since we could play shirtless in a kiddie pool."

Bo laughs and shakes his head. "Yeah, but she's what you've got, and if you have any intention of ever going back to Austin, she'll need to sign off on you."

I rake a hand through my hair, and the

legs of my chair crack as I drop my feet on the deck. "I see her tomorrow. I'll try. I just don't know if I can."

"You could always talk to me, ya know? Best friend, Bo?"

I balance my elbows on my knees and drop my head in my hands. I've got all kinds of offers to talk, but what I can't seem to make anyone understand is that I don't know what to say. I'm grateful for the offers, but it seems like beating my head against a concrete wall.

Instead of saying something hateful, I nod and lean back in the chair. "I know, and if something changes, I'll let you know."

Bo finishes off the taco, reaches down, and digs in the bag for another. He works it over like the last and takes a bite. "Ugh. Not as good as the first."

Laughing, I nod. "Would you have believed me if I'd told you that?"

He flings the wilted lettuce over the

railing and picks at the taco filling. "Probably not. How can the first one taste so good and not the second one?"

"Got me," I say and eye the taco. "I suffered through and ate the second one. I've got a long while until the potluck tonight."

"Martha Goldman is still bringing that god-awful mac and cheese."

My lips curl up. Man, that was nasty stuff. "Who eats it?"

Bo shrugs and looks as dumbfounded as I feel. "I don't know, but the bowl is clean at the end of the dinner every time."

I shake my head, knowing it isn't possible someone is eating it. "Someone has to be raking it into the trash and hiding it to save her feelings. That's the only possible explanation."

Bo throws his head back and laughs. After last night, it's even squishier today.

I can't seem to keep my thoughts from drifting to Uriah. His bright green eyes, electric smile, and throaty laugh tickle my throat and stomach and give me goose-bumps. I rub my arms to try to erase the evidence, but I'm too late.

"You cold?"

I pull my sleeves down and cover my hands with the cuffs. "Not really."

He points to my now-covered arms. "You sure?"

"Yeah."

His phone starts beeping, and he pulls it out of his tailored jacket pocket. "Oh, time for me to go. Short lunch. Got some sixth-graders to impress today."

I look at him funny, wondering why he'd be going to the middle school.

With an exasperated sigh, he replies, "I told Becky Martin I'd come in and talk to the kids. She's doing a section on law in history class."

"She still giving you those looks like she did in high school?" I ask and grin. Now, talk about a crush. That girl had doe eyes anytime Bo was in her vicinity.

Bo cuts his eyes to me like I've broached a sensitive topic. "Yeah."

I smile.

"I can pick you up tonight for the potluck."

"Already got a ride."

He tilts his head as his eyebrow knit together. "Who?"

"Uriah Pendleton."

Bo stands and looks down at me. The way the sun's shining through the trees gives him a halo like he's some angel sent to rescue me, but he's not Uriah. He harrumphs.

"What?" I ask.

"Of course, he's picking you up. He's crushed on you since we were kids."

My mouth drops open. Was I the only person who had no idea? "You knew?"

Bo's blinking as if I've said the dumbest

thing he's ever heard. "You didn't?"

Shaking my head, I say, "No."

Bo shakes his head and rolls his eyes. "Lillian James, you are the most clueless person I've ever known."

That doesn't <u>sit</u> right with me, and I prickle with anger. "Maybe I just didn't want to know. Maybe I wanted to be clueless. You ever think of that? Maybe I thought that if I knew, I couldn't leave this town, and leaving this town was what I needed most at the time."

"Well, you're back now, and those of us left in your wake are still trying to piece together what happened to you and why you left and never came back."

I sigh, and water pools in my eyes. Bo seems to notice, and his stance softens.

"I'm sorry, Lilly," he says and checks his phone again. "I gotta go. I'll see you later."

In my head, I say, *Yeah, later,* and he's gone before I realize I didn't say it out loud.

CHAPTER EIGHT

I spend my day on the deck, watching the birds, listening to the distant creek, and pushing back at the memory trying to crawl its way out of my skull. When I go to take my shower, dark clouds are rolling in again, and I wonder if it'll rain before Uriah arrives to pick me up. That's Texas for ya.

The water isn't set to boiling this time, but it still feels good. I haven't quite put my finger on why the shower in this cabin feels better than any shower I've ever taken. Maybe it's the quiet. Maybe it's the smell of the woods. Or maybe it's just me and I haven't felt clean in such a long time that part of me thinks if I stand under the water long enough, I'll feel squeaky again.

After my shower, I stand by the glass doors in the bedroom. Not a drop of water has fallen outside, but I can taste the rain in the air. The clouds keep getting darker like they're being fed from the memories I'm keeping under lock and key. I lean my forehead against the glass and let the coolness seep in.

Pushing off, I walk back into the bathroom. The fog from my shower has dissipated, and I can see myself in the mirror. Looking in the mirror has been weird for me since I was a kid. Other people tell me they see their reflection, but not me.

What I see when I look in the mirror is fractured. When that happened, I don't know. A pull in my stomach tells me I'm reaching for something I can't quite handle yet. I smile at the person staring back at me and walk away.

Makeup has never been my thing, so I use my time to finger-comb my hair. If I brush it, the humidity will make me look like I've stuck my finger in a socket. It hangs loosely down my back and over my shoulders. The light brown curls bounce as I continue getting some of the bigger tangles out.

I hear the crunch of tires out front and close my eyes. Uriah. The name is like cotton candy on my tongue, melting into my taste buds, and the flavor blankets my mouth, lingering and sugary.

When he knocks on the door, he says, "Hey, Lills, it's me. Are you decent?"

"I'm dressed, if that's what you mean," I yell through the door and pull it open.

He stands there, looking like a cross between G.I. Joe and Ken, and my lips spread into a smile without my permission or approval like my face has a mind of its own. The untucked plaid button-up shirt, boot-cut jeans, and the way the sun has given him an allover tan makes him complete and utter eye candy.

"Hey, Lills," he says and smiles.

I find some words, and they all assemble into a squeaky, "Hi." I fidget with the hem of my shirt and then run my hands down the side of my jeans. I feel like I haven't dressed good enough.

"You look good, Lilly. You look real good."

"You don't look bad yourself. You forget your cowboy hat?"

"No." Uriah laughs and grabs my hand as he pulls me out the door. I still have my hand on the knob, and the movement whiplashes the door shut with a smack. "Come on. I'm hungry."

The short ride to town lends to superficial talk. "This truck isn't nearly as pretty in the daylight," I say.

"Better than walking," replies Uriah.

I raise my eyebrows and cut him a side-look.

"Okay, that applies to most people." He leans forward as he's driving and looks up at the clouds. "And, at least it's dry for when whatever that is decides to sing."

I lean forward too and look up. "Yeah, guess so. Maybe it's just a threat, and we all just need to kneel and pray."

"I don't need threats to kneel and pray."

"How do you know He's talking to you? Maybe other people are deaf."

"You deaf?"

"Nah, I got good hearing. I talk to Papa all the time," I say and continue staring out the windshield.

"That's not what you call your dad?"

"No, it's what I call Jesus."

"You call Jesus 'Papa'?"

"Yeah, so?"

Uriah seems to chew on that for a few moments. He looks at me. "Never heard Him called Papa before."

"Well, now you have."

"I thought you didn't go to church."

"I don't. I don't need to go to church to talk to Papa."

"Have you been talking to Papa? 'Cause I'd think if you had, you wouldn't be here for the next six months," Uriah says and parks the truck in front of the church.

He's thrown a dagger, and it's lodged in my throat. I swallow hard and look away. I've got two choices right now: stay in the truck and fight the tears, or get out of the truck and pretend I didn't hear him. I pick option number two and jump out of the truck.

Uriah makes a mad dash out and joins me as I walk to the church. He laces his fingers in mine, and I jerk my hand away. I stop and turn him to face me. God help me, as cute as he is, I'm gonna set him straight here and now.

"Listen, we haven't talked in a long time. If you want to pick up where we left off, fine, but we left off as friends and nothing more. You hear me, Uriah Pendleton?" My voice has reached an octave I never thought it capable of.

The smile that spreads across his face is warm and wonderful, and I just yelled at the face that makes me all melty. "Okay, Lills, you set the rules, and I'll live by them until I can't."

I narrow my eyes at him, doing my best to look menacing. Well, as menacing as a few hairs over five feet can look. "You're dang right you will."

"Oh, is it a lover's quarrel already?" Misty's voice drips anything but dew.

Before I can say anything, Uriah steps in front of me and partially shields me with his body. "Misty, you go on now. This conversation's not for you."

She glides up to him, her stupid face smiling. "Oh, Uriah, you know me. I'm just playing."

"You're right; I do know you. And you do little in the way of playing. Now, the doors are that way. See yourself to 'em."

Uriah guards me with his arms and turns as Misty walks past. I hide my face in his back. If only I were small enough to hide completely, maybe Misty would just leave me alone once and for all.

He turns to me and takes me by the shoulders to look my face over. "You okay?"

I lift my head, meeting his gaze with my lips pinched together. There should be a reason that girl doesn't like me. "Why does Misty hate me? What did I ever do to her?"

"I don't know, but you don't mind her. Ya hear?"

I take a deep breath and lean my forehead against him. He wraps those cannons around me, and I wish I hadn't set him so straight after all. My iron-clad will to keep him a friend is turning into aluminum foil by the time he lets me go.

"Come on. I smell something good. Can't you?"

I catch a whiff of fresh-baked bread, and my stomach says something like, *Eat a taco and die.*

CHAPTER NINE

Inside the church kitchen slash gymnasium slash extra classrooms, tables of food are lined against the wall, along with rows of tables and chairs.

I watch several ladies, Uriah's and Bo's mommas included, hustling around in the kitchen, stirring food and sticking assorted ladles, forks, and spoons in the offered dishes. Mrs. Pendleton throws a quick wave at Uriah and returns her attention to the buckets of food that have been brought in.

In the back of my mind, I'm remembering church potlucks are also a crap-shoot, and just because it looks good doesn't mean it is good. My eyes land on a pie with my name on it. If I eat nothing else at this thing, that pecan pie is mine. And then I see the ice cream. After my not-so-heavenly fruit bar and tacos this morning, this kitchen is like a veritable smorgasbord making my stomach roll and my mouth water.

Pastor Jeffrey Anderson comes walking in, smiling and shaking hands, and then his eyes land on me. The smile disappears almost too briefly to catch, but I see it. He continues shaking hands and greeting people until he gets to me and Uriah.

"Well, hello, Uriah!" He slaps Uriah on the back and shakes his hand with an exuberance akin to a jumping bean.

Pastor Jeffrey sets his hands on his hips and looks me over. Up, down and down, up. "Hey, there, Lillian." His words pause, but his lips look like they've got other things to say. "How are you?"

I catch sight of Bo, and he sidles up beside his daddy. He's giving me hard looks too.

Bo sticks out his hand to Uriah, and they shake. I'm waiting for them to arm wrestle or bump chests or something, but they drop their hands and just smile at each other.

It gives me time to think for a moment. My brain feels like a mustang rearing and ready to flee. I shrink a little and offer up, "I guess I'm okay." What else am I supposed to say? I can see people casting glances my way, hoping to hear something so hot their lips can't do anything but spread it.

Bo locks eyes with Uriah. "You guys sit at our table, okay?"

Uriah's smile broadens, and he slaps him on the shoulder. "We can do that."

I see the way they're looking at each

other. "Maybe we could get a plate and sit outside," I blurt out.

"Nah, when I came in, rain was falling sideways," Bo says.

Inside, I feel like a coyote caught in a leg trap. There's no point in fighting it. I'm sitting at the preacher's table, and there's not a diddly thing I can do about it.

The place is nearly packed at this point. Pastor Jeffrey whistles like he's calling for a cab, and the room simmers down. He makes a short speech about Jesus, the last supper, and some kind of fundraiser for VBS going on this summer. How he managed to link those three things together is lost on me.

He points his finger and calls on Mr. Marlin. As the man walks past me, his cologne bites my nose, and I nearly double over. That memory, hiding in the folds of my lobes, tries to screech to the front. Uriah says something about the color in my face, but I can't hear him as my heart hammers so hard that all I can hear is *thump, thump, thump.* Finally, someone opens the door, and a blast of wind rips through the room. The smell and memory leave as fast as they hit.

I stare in the direction of Mr. Marlin and frown, not knowing why. Everyone bows their head—except Uriah. I can feel his stare boring a hole in the side of my cheek. Mr. Marlin waits for everyone to close their eyes, and then he steals a glance my way.

Instantly, the hairs on my arms stand up, my head swims, and my breath is caught in my lungs. They feel like they're about to explode by the time I rip my eyes away from his. None of this exchange is lost on Uriah, and I know, I just know, our truck ride home will be filled with questions I can't answer yet.

When Mr. Marlin finishes, he takes his

spot at the front of the buffet, and the rest of us bricks get in line. My appetite seems to have gotten lost somewhere between the lawn and the blessing, but I fill my plate with things that seem safe. I'm still eyeing that pie.

Instead of just taking my plate full of food to the table, I make a beeline for the dessert table with Uriah following behind me. I cut a slice big enough to fill whatever the food lying on the plate won't.

Uriah leans down, his lips inches from my ear, and says, "Is that piece big enough for two?"

I shoot a quick glance at him and cut another slice. He looks at me with laughter in his eyes and a smile on his lips. I slap the second slice of pie on another plate. "There's your piece."

Uriah throws his head back and laughs. His shoulders bounce up and down, and I can't help but laugh with him.

As we walk to the preacher's table, Bo's momma is walking down the other side and sits at the same time we do. I look back over to the kitchen, and Uriah's mom is washing dishes. She looks like she might almost be done, and I watch Mrs. Anderson place her purse in the chair next to hers. That's church-lady speak for "This chair's taken."

Mrs. Anderson looks between me and Uriah and then to Bo. I may not have been in church for the last fifteen years, but I know that look. That look's what you get when you're going with someone and you shouldn't be.

"Lillian, I see you found Uriah."

Uriah speaks up, "Well, actually, I found her. Bumped into her yesterday on the sidewalk."

She looks at Bo, who won't look at me at all. He's told her something, and that something has me in a world of trouble with his momma. If he comes to my cabin for lunch tomorrow, I'm gonna take a switch to him and make him spill as to why his momma keeps giving me the stink eye.

"I hear you had a talk at the school today, Bo," Uriah says. This tension isn't lost on him at all.

Bo finally looks up from his plate. "Yeah, sixth graders."

"How did that go?"

Bo shrugs. "Okay, I guess." For a moment, it seems like whatever unspoken sin I've committed has been forgotten, and Bo's momma pats him on the arm.

"He's been talking at the school since he came back from law school. I'm trying to get him to run for the judge's seat when Judge Kringle retires."

My eyebrows shoot up, and my mouth hangs open. I'm left speechless. Judge Kringle retiring? No way. That man has been a judge since before I was born. I figured he'd up and die of a heart attack as he was pounding his gavel in court. Just out of the blue, he'd keel over, gone.

Bo catches my moment of surprise and smiles a sly grin like he's got more secrets in a box he's just waiting to let loose.

"You thinking about being a judge? Wow, that's impressive," Uriah says.

"I don't know. It's just thoughts for now, but I've got the education and the experience. Clearly, I can negotiate tough cases," Bo says and levels his eyes at me.

My pulse jumps as Bo, his momma, his daddy, and Uriah all look at me. Plus a few people on the outskirts of the conversation. Uriah's momma saves me by sitting right at that moment.

"Hey, y'all," she says and smiles. She reaches over and pats Uriah's hand. "How's my boy?"

"I'm fine, Momma. You look a little tired, though."

"Oh, well, ya know." Her entire demeanor is upbeat and lively. It brings a freshness to the table, for which I'm grateful. The smile she gives me is warm and filled with love. "Hi, Lillian, it's good to see you here."

"Hi, Mrs. Pendleton, how are you?"

"Oh, Jesus smiles on me." Mrs. Pendleton has said that exact statement every time she's replied for as long as I can remember. "How are you?"

I open my mouth to speak, when Misty walks up behind her, places her hands on her shoulders, and plants a kiss on her cheek. Well, Judas was sweet too.

"Hi, Mrs. Pendleton." Misty actually sounds genuine.

Mrs. Pendleton twists in the chair to talk to her. Each time Uriah's momma laughs, Misty's eyes cut to me as if to say, *See, I'm better than you.* She probably is. It's not like she knifed her daddy at the Thriftway.

The last time Misty turns her eyes to me, I can see her twisty little brain working the hamster overtime. She smiles all sweet, looks at me doe-eyed, and then lowers the verbal boom. "How's your daddy, Lillian?"

Of course, she picked the moment I'd taken a drink. The color drains from my face as I choke and stutter. I have no idea how my daddy's doing. I haven't seen him, heard from him, spoken to him, or anything since that day. I don't even know if he's been released from the hospital yet.

Mrs. Pendleton looks at me, her eyes full of nothing but love and forgiveness. She looks back up at Misty, not seeming to understand why she'd be so hateful to me. "George is just fine. He got out this morning, and Mrs. Buckner said he's on the mend. Now, you run along, Misty Morning, before your mouth gets you in trouble with Jesus."

Whoa. New and profound love doesn't seem to cover how I feel for Mrs. Pendleton right at this moment. I try to smile, but my lips wiggle, and I feel like I might cry.

She reaches over to pat my hand and then takes a bite of mac and cheese. "Now, as I was walking up to the table, I heard that Bo is thinking of being a judge," she says. The topic has been changed, and I'm in the clear for the rest of the evening.

Pastor Jeffrey stands at the table and starts his preaching. No point in moving spots when he's got the ears of the whole joint listening. Besides, why risk some not quite making it to the sanctuary.

CHAPTER TEN

Just as I suspected, the ride to the cabin is spent with Uriah asking me about my reaction to Mr. Marlin.

"What happened tonight?" he asks.

"I don't know."

"How can you not know?" His voice rises on the last word.

"I don't know."

Glancing at me, his eyebrows are knitted together. "Have you reacted that way before?"

I think for a moment. He was at Kettlefish. "No, I saw him at the bar yesterday, and I thought nothing of it."

"Then what made you look like you were gonna puke?" He throws me another glance.

I shake my head and look out the window. Something in the back of my mind itches, and I rub my temples to scratch it. Replaying the moment, I smell the cologne, see his scraggly face and those eyes, and I feel the same visceral reaction. My whole body shivers, but I still can't put together why. My pecan pie is tickling the back of my throat, and I swallow hard to push it back down.

"Lills?"

Somehow, we've driven all the way to my cabin and parked, and I was so caught up in trying to remember that I didn't even notice. "I'm fine." I pull the handle and open the door, and water splashes to my knees when my feet hit the ground.

Uriah is out of the truck just as quickly as I am. He walks me to the door.

I make a face and stomp my foot, water sloshing from my shoes. "Dang it. I forgot to go grocery shopping."

"Did you forget, or did you just not want to go to Thriftway?"

The scene from my last visit flashes. "I don't want to go to that store."

Uriah looks down at his watch. "It closes in twenty minutes. Stay here. I'll be back in thirty."

"You don't—" I start to say, but he's gone before I can finish, so I turn and go inside. The heat seems to be okay. With the moon covered by the rain clouds, the house is so dark it's spooky.

I guess I don't have to worry about my PJs being too thin. It's not like Uriah could see anything anyway. I go to the bathroom, dry myself off, and then switch clothes.

The rain has stopped, so I grab a towel

and walk out onto the deck to dry my chair off before plopping down. I rest my feet on the railing and open-mouth suck in the moist air. It's sharp and crisp and clean. It makes my lungs feel like I'm breathing in ice.

"Papa," I say out loud, "I feel alone. I feel like you've left, and now I'm here alone in this town." I feel a tug on my heart, and Uriah's face springs to my mind. "Sure, I know. He's here, but I feel like it's too late. We had our moment, and it's gone."

The thoughts and feelings ping around in my head until I hear tires. Uriah doesn't bother knocking this time, and he grumbles when he hits his shin on the corner of the entry table. "Don't you have any lights?"

"It's why I needed to go to the store." I come off the deck, turn the light on, and one little light bulb tries to pierce the darkness. It's enough that we can see to put the groceries up, though.

"Why didn't you say something?"

I shrug. "Just forgot. Besides if I had, you left too fast for me to say anything."

"Yeah, guess I did. I'll try to remember to bring you some next time I stop by." Uriah's digging through the bags he carried in. "Here, I thought you could use this." He hands me a little devotional.

I look over the cover and smile. "Thanks. Did you buy this at the store?"

"No, I stopped at the house on my way back. It's one of Momma's. I thought you could read it."

I flip the little book open, and I can see Mrs. Pendleton has used this little book often. She's made little notes and pen marks, and sentences are underlined. Maybe some of her wisdom can leap off the pages and settle in my mind. "You sure your momma won't mind?"

"Shouldn't, since she's the one that picked it out."

The genuineness of the gesture almost brings me to tears. They had both been the kindest to me so far. Not that I've had crosses burned in my yard, but when you've got accusations and judgment thrown your way, you feel it in your marrow.

Uriah empties the last bag and finishes putting up my groceries. I've paid no mind to where things have gone, so tomorrow should be fun, seeing what all he got. "You wanna sit on the deck with me a while, Uriah?"

My offer catches him off guard. He turns to the fridge and pulls out two long-neck bottles. Turns out, he thought I might have a craving for grape soda, and he bought two six-packs. He pops the caps off and hands me one. The grape scent reaches my nose, and I smile. He remembered it was my favorite when we were kids.

I take my chair, lean back, and cross my ankles on the railing. Sitting like this makes me feel relaxed. I'm taking in the sights, forgetting my woes, and just enjoying Papa's big wide world. Even if it is dark, wet, and spooky.

Uriah mirrors me by putting his feet on the railing. We sit quietly for a while. Before long, the crickets and frogs have come out, and they're singing up a storm, no pun intended.

Breaking the silence, Uriah says, "So, I have six months to get to know you again. Why don't we pick up where we left off in the truck when we got to church? Tell me about this Papa thing you do."

I put the bottle to my lips and take a long fizzy drink. "I talk to Papa. I don't know much else I can say."

"What made you start calling Him Papa, though?"

I take a deep breath and let it out slowly. Uriah is looking at me. I can't see him clearly, but I can sure feel it. "It was a few years ago. I was going to this home-group thing, and one night it just kinda hit me. It had been a few years since I'd been here or seen Daddy, and I felt so lonely. The name just flitted into my mind, and it was like He was talking to me. I started calling Him Papa, and it took. I've called Him that ever since."

"But you don't go to church. Isn't it hard to not have fellowship?"

"Who says I haven't had fellowship? Papa says where two or more are gathered, He's there too. We're fellowshippin', aren't we? Talking about Papa, listenin' to His songs," I say and point to the woods. "Papa doesn't need buildings and potlucks and crowds. He just needs us and our willingness to listen and love on Him."

Uriah clears his throat. "Lills, you always did have a way with words."

"I don't have a way with nothin'." I take a

drink and fix my eyes on what I hope is a tree in the distance.

"That's not true, and you know it."

"I don't know nothin' either."

Uriah's chair legs hit the deck, and he scoots himself closer. I can feel the heat coming from him, and it pulls my attention to the fact that it's kinda chilly. "Lills, look at me."

"No."

"Come on. Look at me."

"Why? It's dark. Not like I can see any-thing. Neither can you."

"There's enough light from the kitchen that I can make out a few things, and so can you."

The Borg in my head says resistance is futile, and I drag my eyes to his. "What? What do you need to say that needs my di-rect attention?"

Uriah's face is soft in what little light there is. He brushes my hair off my shoulder and looks at me in a way that makes my bones feel all doughy like I could be baked and served with butter.

"I don't know what happened to you, Lills. It breaks my heart to see you hurt so bad. I know we haven't talked in a really long time, but I love you now just as much as I did back then. I should have protected you from whatever did this to you," Uriah says, his voice so soft and earnest it makes me ache.

"Uriah, I was serious. I'm broken. My pieces are jagged and good for nothin'." I try to keep the desperation I feel out of my voice, but it wavers.

"You know, for someone who talks to Papa so much, you sure don't listen too good."

I sniffle and drink the rest of my soda. "What would you know?"

"Psalm 118:5 says, 'And in my anguish, I

cried out unto the Lord and He rescued me by setting me free.'"

Something inside me breaks. The dam of tears I thought I'd already spilled come pouring down my cheeks quicker than I can swipe them away. Uriah gathers me in his arms, and I can't do anything but cry on his shoulder.

Oh, Papa, where have I been that I've been so deaf?

The tears pour even harder, if that's possible. I grab on to Uriah with all my might, and he holds me even tighter. Maybe my pieces aren't so jagged that he and Papa can't fix them.

CHAPTER ELEVEN

"I feel like I've done this before," I say, sitting in the chair across from Chrissy.

"Maybe it wouldn't feel that way if you'd actually talk about something," she says with a look of concern.

"Where'd you learn that face? College?"

She rolls her eyes and scoffs at me. "Lillian James, if I didn't have a 'Dr.' sitting in the front of my name, I'd take you over my knee and give you a walloping."

"You better hope your daddy was kin to

Hulk; otherwise, you'll have a good ole fight on your hands."

Chrissy looks at me stone-faced and then busts out laughing. "That mouth of yours is going to land you in prison or a coffin one day."

"If I've got a choice, I'll choose the coffin."

She just looks at me, the laughter in her face gone. The silence starts to feel heavy, and Chrissy leans back in her chair. "Lilly, how about we change the way we're doing things? How about you just talk about whatever you want, and we'll go from there?"

I give her a hard look. "You know everything there is to know about me." It's not true, but I hope she buys it.

Chrissy levels her eyes at me, and I know her dollars aren't buying what I got. "Start with after you left here. Where did you go? What did you do?"

There isn't enough air in this awful, earth-colored room to fill up my lungs, but I try anyway. "I went to college when I left, just like all of you."

"Where? No one knew where. Not even your dad."

"No one needed to know."

"Did you go because your momma had just died?"

My jagged pieces grow like Magic Rocks at the mention of my momma. I start to open my mouth and spew something so nasty Papa might blush, but Chrissy cuts me off.

"Don't you start. You're here and I'm here, and what you say won't go anywhere, Lilly. I'm a good listener. Great even. I had a 3.8 GPA in school, and I knocked my doctorate out quicker than anyone in my class. This is my calling. It's what God gave me. So keep your nastiness to yourself."

Chrissy puts water in my gas tank, and

all my hatefulness sputters as tears pool in my eyes. I feel Papa poke my heart with a sharp finger. "I'm sorry, Chrissy." I can't look at her, but the apology is real.

"It's okay, Lilly."

"No, it's not. I got a viper for a tongue sometimes."

"At least you know it," she says, and the laugh that escapes her is light and free. "Now, tell me something. Something with importance. Tell me secrets worth keeping."

I lift my head and stare at her forehead. Meeting her eyes is more than I can handle right now. "I left Foaming Springs because I had to, and I didn't want anyone I knew to be where I was going."

Chrissy sits quiet, doing her therapist thing.

"Everybody knows my biological parents were druggies. They'd come back to town from time to time, but they'd never stay. I was adopted by my biological daddy's parents when I was four, and they were my momma and daddy because they were all I really knew. We were okay while I was little, but as I got older, it got harder. They didn't understand me, and I didn't understand them. Anyone on the outside saw a little family, but on the inside, we were at war."

Chrissy is using her pen, scratching across the paper fast and furious. For a second, I rev my viper and get ready, but then I remember Papa's sharp poke and put it in neutral. She looks up from her clipboard and smiles. "Keep going."

"Me and Momma didn't see eye to eye. She had plans for me, and at no time did she need input from me. I was traveling the world, you see, by any means necessary, whether by military or sugar daddy. I was going to see things she hadn't. Coming up poor made Momma a little crazy about things."

I paused a moment and then continue. "Her dying hurt, but not like an I-missed-her hurt. It hurt because I wanted a relationship with her like other girls had with their mommas. I wanted her to brush my hair, kiss my scars, and want for me what I wanted, but she never could. She loved me," I say, thinking back hard, trying to remember if I believe what I'm saying.

"You okay, Lilly?"

Chrissy's voice rocks me from my memories, and I look at her. "Obviously not. I'm here, aren't I?"

"You know what I mean. Your momma loved you. I saw the way she cared."

"Yeah, I think she did. I think she just loved me the way she thought she wanted to be loved when she was my age. Only, I needed to be loved like I wanted to be loved. Her loving didn't feel like loving. So, when she passed, it was like 'Momma died. The end.' I didn't really feel anything but an emptiness where her body used to be."

"Do you miss her?"

I think for a moment. I want to answer Chrissy honestly, but I haven't been asked that question before, so I don't know the answer just off the top of my head. "No."

"You don't miss your momma?" Chrissy tilts her head, and her eyebrows shoot up like it's the strangest thing she's ever heard.

I give her a stern look. "I thought therapists weren't supposed to judge."

Her posture softens. "We don't, but we do challenge you."

"So, you're challenging my response?"

"I am."

"Why?"

"So you have to back it up with a reason. That way when you think about it the next time, it's not just a feeling or an answer. It's something tangible you can understand. That's what I do. I'm not just a friend sipping coffee with you, taking your answers as gospel. I'm the little voice in the back of your mind, pushing you to really answer the questions and work through what you're actually feeling."

I take a deep breath. "I don't miss my momma. I miss what I could have had with her. If you can miss what you don't even understand."

"Have you tried to understand it?"

I shrug. "I think so. I don't know. I haven't had to think about it, ever."

"Well," Chrissy says and looks at her watch, "we'll be doing three sessions a week starting on Monday, so think about it between now and then. I want a solid answer when you come back. That's your homework."

"I hate homework."

Chrissy smiles. "Maybe you won't by the time you come back."

"Maybe, but don't count on it." I sit for a

moment longer and then push out of the chair.

Oh, Papa, I got mountains that need moving if you're so inclined.

I stuff my hands in my pockets and set off with determination to get light bulbs from Thriftway. My determination turns to cowardice as I round the corner and the sign blinks at me from the distance.

I don't need light bulbs that bad. I spin on my heels in the direction of my woodland cabin.

A truck rumbles next to me, and Uriah pokes his head out the window and smiles. "Why didn't you tell me you needed a ride to town today?"

Why? Because. I've got no good answer beyond just because, so I shrug in response.

"You wanna take a ride and get a bite to eat in the next town over?"

"Can't. Bad girls gotta eat tacos or fish or nuke Hungry Man meals."

"Well, want fish?" he teases.

I walk to the truck and lean my hip against the door.

"She doesn't like fish!" Bo yells from behind me. He jogs to a stop next to the pickup. Those eyes he's got are throwing daggers and large furniture in my direction. His suit is fine and tailored and obnoxious. I wish I could push him in a puddle.

"What you doin', Bo?" Uriah asks.

"Oh, just got some papers to get notarized. Fancy said she'd do it. I've just gotta go to Kettlefish to do it," Bo answers and looks at his watch.

Uriah gives Bo a questioning look. "Why don't you just go to the courthouse to get stuff notarized?"

Bo's lips twist, and he shakes his head. "Because Tallulah Moore is still the court clerk and the only notary. She's just as nasty as when she was a substitute teacher when we were kids, and I avoid her at all costs. I'd rather go to Fancy. She's tough, but she's not nasty."

"I understand that." Uriah nods, and his face scrunches as he looks skyward. "You have lunch yet?"

Now, Papa, I know you're a cunning fellow, but this idea is sounding about as good as sticking my hand in a dark hole, hoping to pull out a catfish. What if there's a snake in there?

Bo looks at me and then at Uriah and then at me again. He's thinking the same thing I am, only he's not hiding it as well. "I don't know."

"Oh, come on. We're friends, me and you. How many times did I help you tip the cows in your grandma's field?"

Bo laughs at the memory. A memory I'm absent in. "All right. Where?"

Uriah looks at me. "Lady's choice."

"Tish's. Just don't want them cold ever again."

"Okay, I'll meet you two there." Bo looks

at his watch again and sprints in the direction of Kettlefish, and I walk around the front of the pickup and hop in. If I'm going, I may as well ride.

The truck rumbles as Uriah hits the gas pedal. It chugs along, and he's humming a hymn I recognize: "All to Jesus I Surrender."

There you go again, Papa. That finger you got seems extra sharp today. I rub the spot on my chest directly over my heart. I hear the little voice that seems to be growing louder the longer I'm in town.

Papa says, *Sometimes my finger needs to be extra pointy; otherwise, no one listens.*

I can feel the tears burning to be released, but I blink a few times. That seems to quell the tide in my eyes, and I decide the silence isn't what I want right now. "Why'd you invite Bo?"

Uriah stops humming. "Why not?"

"You didn't see the looks he was giving me?"

"I saw them. I want him to confront them. I want him to see you and stop being jealous. I want him to move on and find someone who will love him. If we keep just tossing him aside, we let his anger grow and fester, and we can't do that. It's not what Jesus, or Papa, would want."

Well, dang. "Okay. Point taken."

CHAPTER TWELVE

Bo slides into the seat next to me. Uriah has ordered enough tacos that I believe them to be in my foreseeable breakfast future.

I slide a bag to Bo. "No lettuce this time," I say.

He bumps me with his shoulder and smiles. "You know me so well."

"So, what Friday plans have you got for tomorrow?" Uriah directs the question to Bo.

Bo unwraps his taco and takes a bite before answering. "I thought I'd go to the town over and see a show. They've got a run of old movies playing."

"The drive-in?" Uriah asks.

"Yeah, should be fun. What are you doing?"

"I'd like to go with you if you've got the room."

Bo looks taken aback. I'm taken aback. We got abacks flying left and right. I look at them with wide eyes, eating my taco, keeping my mouth full.

"Well, you got someone special you're taking, or can I come?" Uriah chomps down on his chicken taco, and a strip hangs down his chin. I can't help but snicker as he pushes it into his mouth and gives me a smile.

"No, I'm not taking anyone special. You mean you aren't spending every waking moment with Lilly?"

My strategy to keep food in my mouth

backfires, and I choke. I take a sip of soda to stop the hacking.

Uriah comes to my rescue, though. "Lilly needs Lilly time, and I need guy time with someone I considered a good friend before I left for the service."

Lilly needs Lilly time. I do have homework. Stupid homework.

Bo twists to look at me. "Well, she certainly can't go. Judge Kringle has her on lockdown in Foaming Springs."

"Told you bad girls don't have options," I say without looking at either of them.

"You're not a bad girl," Bo says, and Uriah bounces his head up and down in agreement.

"No? What's your definition of a bad girl, then?" In my mind, I feel like I fill that definition quite well with a big red letter "B" written on my chest.

"There are bad girls, and then there's a girl who's made a bad choice," Uriah says.

"You definitely made a bad choice. No argument there," Bo adds.

I slouch and look at the wall. "Well, I can't argue either," I whisper, but I know they've heard me.

Uriah reaches across the table and smacks Bo on the arm. "You remember that time Lilly went missing in the woods?"

My rear burns a little from the memory of the punishment, and I shift in the booth.

"Yeah, man, her momma paddled her something fierce. Right there at the edge of the woods, in front of the whole town. Lilly looked like she had no idea what was happening," Bo says like he's recalling the whole scene.

"I don't know if she got paddled for going missing or the way she talked to her momma after she was found."

"Both," I interject.

"You always did have a mouth." Bo shakes his head. "I was lucky you kept quiet in front of Judge Kringle, or you may not be sitting here."

"I didn't have anything to say."

"Yeah, but when you do, it's worth hearing most of the time." Uriah smiles as he looks at me.

"Did your dad ever whip you like that?" Bo asks. I don't think he's thought through the question, because the look on his face makes me think he regrets asking.

My head hurts all of a sudden, like fireworks with a bad fuse busting inside my skull. "Sometimes, but most of the time he didn't have to whip me. He just used words with a surgeon's precision."

"I didn't know that, Lilly," Uriah says just above a whisper.

"Don't. Don't give me those looks." I turn my head to the wall. "I don't need your sympathy or your sweetness or anything." Anger bubbles in my throat like fizzy soda. "This is why I never told anyone. I got what

I got, and that was all there was to it. Not like anyone could have done anything, and I can't change it now."

The three of us sit in silence. It's horrible and uncomfortable, and it smells like toe jam socks. I wish I'd kept my mouth shut. Why didn't I? It's not like saying this stuff can change anything.

"How did your momma handle your dad?"

That's a new question. I search my memories like an old library card catalog. "I don't remember."

"Do you know what happened to your biological parents? Did they ever try to contact you after you were adopted?"

"Some. My biological daddy, Will, did, of course, 'cause he was Momma's baby boy. I only met Uncle Robert, my momma's other son, a few times. When I was four, right before I was adopted, Lucy, my biological momma, kidnapped me. She got as far as West Virginia, and I was gone two or three months. Can't remember for sure now." It pops out like hot kernels in an iron skillet. I slap my hand over my mouth, not knowing why I said it.

Bo and Uriah react like I expect them to. The town may have known I was adopted, but few knew Lucy had taken me. It's not like Momma and Daddy talked about it. Not from what I remember anyway.

"What?" they ask in unison.

It's out now, and I shrug because, to me, it's not big news. I've lived with it so long that it doesn't even feel real anymore. It never really occurred to me to say anything before now. What difference did it make?

"What did your momma and daddy do? Did your biological dad do anything?" Bo asks.

Uriah's green eyes are studying me hard. He's both shocked and heart-hurt for me at the same time.

"They hired a private investigator and prayed. The private investigator never could find me, but eventually, the FBI did. After they got me back, they made the adoption official. Lucy wrote a couple times when I got older, but I was mad at her. If she'd wanted to talk to me, maybe she should have hung around. I don't know where she is now, and I have no inclination to go searching for her."

They both seem to reel from the revelation. Uriah's eyebrows raise, and Bo just looks at me like I've eaten a worm. They asked, and I answered. What's the big deal?

"So, your biological dad, he hung around?" Bo askes.

"Do you remember seeing him?" I ask.

Shrugging, Bo answers, "A few times."

"Well, there ya go. A few times. He came around, spent a couple of nights, and in a flash of false promises, he was gone. He died about six years ago. Daddy called and told me."

"Wow. Why did you keep all this to yourself?" Uriah is genuine when he asks.

I throw my hands up. "I don't know. It never dawned on me that it was something worth telling. Being taken wasn't the worst of what's happened to me, and it's just a way for people to talk about things they know nothing of. Can we just stop talking about it now? Please? Besides, if I spill all my secrets here, Chrissy might just feel useless."

They chuckle nervously, and that seems to change the topic and the mood. Uriah and Bo start planning their trip to the drive-in, and I sit quietly, wondering how it's going to be with a full weekend alone with myself.

CHAPTER THIRTEEN

Uriah drives me home, but he doesn't stay. His momma has a list of things for him to do, and my mood doesn't really make for a lot of room in my little cabin. I change clothes, grab a grape soda, and take up residence on the deck.

It's sunny and bright, and the birds are dipping and diving. Woody is nowhere to be seen, but I've got a squirrel eyeing me. He has a buddy, and they start playing in the trees, their little bushy tails swishing as they leap from tree to tree.

My thoughts start to wander back to Tish's. I'm happy all those bags of tacos Uriah bought weren't for me. Apparently, there are a few families in town that he's been dropping in and giving food to. He's sweeter than sugar.

I mentally whoop myself for telling those two about being taken by Lucy. I try to picture Lucy's face, and I can't. She's been gone so long that her face and memory are just faded, and there's no picture.

The breeze picks up and whips through my clothes. The air has turned icy, and goosebumps line my arms like a little army. My toes tingle from the bite of the wind, but I don't want to move. I want to sit here on the deck with the frosty breeze and watch the sun as it moves across the sky.

I take a sip of my soda and wiggle my toes, and then Papa decides to take a seat next to me. More than anything, I wish He would take a vacation and leave me alone for a little while. I still need a Band-Aid from the last time He poked me with His sharp finger.

He sits quietly for a while, smiling in my direction, letting me stew. Then He pounces with the grace of an elephant. My heart itches and tingles and hurts and bleeds.

"Why did you let this stuff happen to me?" I ask out loud to my audience of birds, squirrels, and Papa. I feel Papa more than the birds and squirrels. "Why couldn't you just let me be normal? What did I do to deserve all the crud that's happened to me? I didn't ask to be born. You put me on this earth, and now look at me. I'm all warped and twisted."

Tears spring to my eyes. I feel the hurt all the way down to my soul. The kind of hurt that just rips and shreds and leaves nothing but tattered pieces lying all over.

A cry slips between my teeth and out my lips. I jump out of the chair, walk to the corner of the deck, and take in a new view. There's a part of me that wants to fling myself off the railing, but I know I'd just end up with a few broken bones. Then I'd have to explain myself, and that seems like more trouble than the broken bones.

My lips tremble, and I brush my hand across the waterfall running down my face. "I'm alone, you know. I'm all alone."

Papa cups my heart and blows cool air on it, trying to put out the burning fire. It's His way of saying I'm not alone.

"But I am. I am alone. I got you, but no one on this earth. You hear me?" I yell the question into the expanse of the forest like a lion growling on the savanna.

Papa squeezes my insides like He's trying to hug me, but I feel like my muffin's getting busted.

"If they knew my dark parts, they'd

never talk to me again. All that blackness that covers me like an oil slick would just ooze out onto them too. Then they'd be all black and ugly and worthless…" I choke on the last word. It comes out in sputters and spits.

Then another realization hits me with the force of a tidal wave. Uriah can't fix me. My fence is in splinters, and you just can't fix that kind of damage. You just have to start over. I don't know what hurts worse, me being all ugly blackness or the fact that Uriah deserves better than me.

"Papa, why'd you do this?" I look in the direction of where Papa is sitting. I see His face. He's smiling and welcoming, and all I can think is I want to just pound on Him. I don't want Him smiling at me. I'm so mad now.

"Why did you have to let him bump into me? Why? Don't you love him, too? Don't you know he needs better than the trash heap I am?"

Papa speaks calmly. "I love Uriah just as much as I love you. You think you're the only one that prays and asks for answers? He prayed for you, and I answered him."

"But why does he want me? I'm no good. I stab daddies in Thriftway."

Papa sits quietly. Those squirrels He's fashioned feel Him here too. They dance like I've never seen before. The birds join in too. A new lighter, cooler breeze blows. It touches my face, and it's like Papa is caressing my tears away. But I'm not ready for niceness.

"Why you gotta be like this? I'm not ready for all this stuff. I don't want to deal with all this. I came here to visit Daddy and leave. Why did you let me do that? Why'd you let me get myself in trouble? I thought you were my friend. I thought you loved me. I thought you wanted good things for me. I thought..." My ugly cry comes back even more vicious, and I kneel in the corner of the deck and bow my head. The wounds split open, pus pours out, and I just can't do anything but lean back against the rickety railing and hope it doesn't break.

My pain is like a disease I can't find a cure for, and I cry. I cry for the life I think I should have had, for the parents I wanted, for the grandparents I needed, and for all the things I think Papa has stolen from me.

I cry.

And I cry.

And I cry some more.

By the time I stop crying, I can feel Papa telling me He loves me and He'll be back later. I don't know what later means, but I understand. My company right now is utterly horrible, and I wouldn't want to sit with me either.

Papa says, "I'm not leaving because you're bad company. I always love you. I love you enough to give you someone you think is too good for you. I love you enough to give you trials and heartbreak because when it's all over, you'll be my shining glory, and anyone and everyone looking your direction will see my fingers everywhere in your life."

"Why you gotta be so nice to me? Surely my jagged pieces are enough to cut you too. Besides, can't people see your glory without me stabbing the man who raised me?"

An Aaron Shust song springs to mind. No, no I'm definitely not skilled to understand what God has willed or what God has planned. The song plays like a lullaby in my head as Papa gives me space.

CHAPTER FOURTEEN

When I woke up this morning, I had no intention whatsoever of stepping foot in this church for the Sunday service, but here I am, steppin' and sittin'. I take a spot in a pew in the back of the church in the far corner with the hope that I'm ignored until the service is over.

Papa gets a dirty look from me when I cast my eyes skyward for a moment. Why He made me come is lost on me. What can I get here that I can't get in the cabin? *I know where you live, ya know,* I say to Him in my head.

I feel Him settle over me and my spirit.

"Fine," I mumble under my breath. "I'm here, but I don't have to be happy about it." I cross my arms over my chest and slouch down in the seat.

Uriah is walking down the aisle to the front of the church when he looks back over his shoulder and sees me. I guess absence makes the heart grow fonder because the smile he flashes me is something worthy of an Olympic medal. The girly parts of my brain squeal in delight. The other two percent yell at it to shut up.

As he continues walking to the front of the church, I look for who might be the recipient of all Uriah has to offer, and I see Misty. I feel like someone has come along and stolen all my air. My head feels light.

My brain starts yelling at me, and this time the girly parts and the not-so-girly parts gang up on me. You said he deserved better than you, remember? I don't know who's asking, me or Papa. Surely, if he deserves better than me, he deserves better than Misty too.

While watching him talk to her, Jenny Walman joins them. Misty cuts her eyes in my direction, and the smile greeting me is anything but sweet or friendly. Shots have been fired over my bow, and I'm sinking into the ocean. Jenny waves, and I limply wave back.

Uriah is waving at me to come join them, and I flat-out refuse. My butt is planted in this corner, and unless he has pie, I'm not moving. I shake my head a few times and then look down to avoid his insistence.

I guess he took the hint because when I look the next time, he's sauntering in my direction and sits next to me. "You coulda come and said hello."

"Didn't want to lose my spot." I pretend I'm reading an old bulletin.

"You didn't want to deal with Misty." He bumps me with his shoulder and chuckles.

"That too." I flick a glance at him.

"She's not horrible."

I can't help but drop the bulletin in my lap and look at him. "Then explain to me what I did to make her hate me. I never did anything to her, but she's sure gone out of her way to make sure I know she doesn't like me."

Uriah sits quietly.

That's right, soldier, you got nothing. "See. Even you don't have an answer."

He shrugs. "Have you ever thought about sitting your butt down and asking her?"

"Mice don't ask the cat why it's hungry. They just go down smooth with ketchup." I don't dare look in him in the eyes. There's a good chance I'd march over and do what he says, and I am in no mood to deal with Misty.

Uriah bounces with laughter. "I don't know if I can sit by you during church. If I laugh while Pastor Jeffrey is preaching, he'll probably take me out behind the shed and wear me out."

I pull out a hymnal I know I'll need soon and ask, "Wouldn't he have to catch you first?"

"Seriously, Lilly, maybe you should just sit down with Misty one day and ask. Maybe you did something and didn't even realize it and it hurt her feelings." His tone is serious and genuine. He has a peacemaker's spirit.

"What if she just hates me because she's a mean, vindictive, hag of a girl and her lot in life is to pester me until I'm dead?"

"Then at least you'll know, and you won't have to wonder anymore. Maybe you might have a good friend that loves you after all's said and done."

I snort. "Sure. Me and Misty, friends. That'll be the day."

"You never know. Isn't *Papa* all about miracles?" He makes a point to emphasize Papa.

"Walking on water would be easier than being friends with Misty."

People are filing in now. I haven't been here since I got into town, so anyone who hasn't already seen me on Wednesday makes their trek over to hug me and tell me hi.

See, Papa, this is why I didn't want to come to church. I hear His light, happy laugh, and it tickles my heart. *Ugh, Papa, just stop.*

Pastor Jeffrey takes to the pulpit, and everyone hushes. He bows his head and says a prayer, and then Jenny gets up and leads the singing. I should have known that sugary pile of bones would lead the singing.

She asks us to stand, and inwardly I groan, but I do it so I don't have to deal with Uriah giving me grief.

We sit, stand, sing, stand, sit, pray, and then Pastor Jeffrey gets up to the pulpit again and pulls out his Bible from a hidden cubbyhole. He flips it open and tells everyone to turn to Romans 1:28-32. The title of his sermon is "Loving Evil Instead of Good."

I know he's talking to me when he looks at me, and then Bo, sitting next to his momma, turns to stare right at me. He's not just talking to me; he's talking about me. I'm the evil. All I wanna do is hide.

Uriah must feel my readiness to flee because he puts a hand on my knee and gives me a look that says stay put. He leans over, his lips next to my ear, and says, "I've got you."

He pulls back, and his eyes lock with mine. Then he turns his attention to the rest of the church. His eyes narrow, his jaw flexes, and the look on his face lets everyone there know he means business.

Mrs. Pendleton is looking too, only she's beaming at Uriah. Her boy has done exactly what she's taught him to do: be brave when the whole world is throwing rocks.

If Pastor Jeffrey has anything else to say to me today, he'll have to do it in private. Uriah Pendleton has spoken without saying a word, and it was loud enough for everyone to hear.

My shoulders sag, I put my head down, and I wish like I've never wished before that Papa will bring someone worthy of Uriah, because I am not her. I know I'm not. My darkness is bleeding outside the edges, getting Uriah messy. I feel ashamed and rotten.

CHAPTER FIFTEEN

Uriah asks me to lunch after church, but I don't want to stay in town. He says I can come eat with him and his momma, but I don't want that either. The idea that I could spread my trash in her house just bugs the tar out of me.

He reluctantly drops me off at the cabin, and I disappear into the house instead of watching him drive away. I wonder if I could watch him drive away if I knew he was never coming back. The thought slaps me hard.

I switch out of my church clothes into my pajamas and take my place outside. It's just me and the woods again until the movie projector in my head starts replaying the events at church.

Pastor Jeffrey in his Sunday best, Bo in his even better Sunday best, his momma with her stiff posture, and the entire congregation twisting their necks to look at my train wreck.

Tell me again, Papa, how going to church was good for me.

I stew and chew, getting mad and madder and maddest still. I'm steaming before long. Those people don't know me. They know what I show them. They know what they think they know and nothing more. They throw stones at my glass house and think the stones pass through their own glass houses without causing any damage.

The birds have stopped singing, and the

squirrels are staring at me with their little beady eyes.

"What, you haven't seen anyone mad before?" I ask them.

They just keep looking at me, tails twitching.

I pad into the kitchen, pull out a soda, and pop the top off. The cool liquid rolls down my throat, cold and frothy. I carry it out to the deck along with a bag of chips that was stashed in a cabinet.

My anger is simmering at the top of my pot, and I can feel the water about to boil over. I open the bag of chips, pop one in my mouth, and chase it with a swig of the soda.

Papa comes sliding in and casually sits next to me.

"I'm in no mood to play, Papa."

He doesn't say anything, so we sit in silence while I eat my chips and drink my soda.

April is such a moody month, I think as an

almost warm breeze blows by. The thought strikes me as funny because I've been so moody. I begin to laugh, and it turns into a cackle. Now that I'm laughing, I can't seem to turn it off. I'm still mad and giggling like my jackets should come in white and buckle in the back.

Papa still sits quietly.

I look at Him, laughing my head off, drinking my soda and eating my chips. I've gone nuts.

"Papa, what am I to do about that homework?" I ask, still laughing like an idiot. "Why don't I miss Momma?"

The laughter dies in my throat. The sobering thought wipes all my funny away. I want to know the answer to the question as much as Chrissy does, but I don't know the answer.

"Why, Papa? Tell me why?"

Papa is eerily quiet. Maybe He doesn't know the answer either.

I feel a sharp prick in my heart, and I try to think real hard about Momma. It's been a long time since I've thought of her.

She died. The end.

I wrack my brain, trying to think about why her death doesn't bother me. It should. The woman raised me as her own, gave me food and shelter, snuggled me at night.

"Wait," I say out loud. "She didn't snuggle me at night."

My head hurts. All this thinking and laughing and being mad has given me a headache that makes my eyes want to bleed. I try to remember if I've got any meds for it and go to my room and rummage in the nightstand drawer. The bottle is childproof, but I slip the top off with ease and pop two of them in my mouth and take a drink of my soda.

I pad back into the kitchen. Those chips just aren't doing it for me. The cabinets are stocked with all sorts of canned goods. I find bread, peanut butter, and jelly and go for one of the simple things in life: a PB&J.

Back out on the deck, with my sandwich and another soda, I'm in a frame of mind to not think. If only it were that simple.

Papa is still sitting in the chair. Still waiting for me to find an answer to a question I didn't even know I had until I got back to my hometown.

I finish my sandwich before I do any real thinking because, for once, I'd like to eat a meal in peace. The peanut butter sticks in my teeth, and I take a long drink. Man, Uriah really knew what he was doing when he bought these sodas. I sure hope I can save one for him for the next time he's here.

Clouds are rolling in, and I can smell rain in the air. These evening showers are nice, and I know Texas needs the rain. All that thinking I've been putting off comes rolling in too.

Papa's been waiting.

"Why don't I miss my momma? Why doesn't it hurt like the dickens when I think about her being gone?" I ask out loud. Maybe the birds or the squirrels or something in the distance can give me an answer.

I certainly don't have an easy answer.

Nothing about this question feels easy either. I play the memories I have of Momma and me together. She only busted me really bad once or twice. Most of the time, she played referee between me and Daddy.

I start to touch on a memory of Daddy and force it back. I can only deal with one devil at a time. Momma's face floats to the front. I see her smile.

Momma and Daddy were older when they adopted me. In pictures of when Momma was young, she always looked sad, even when she was smiling. Daddy was her third husband. She told me he was a rough man when they met, and by my thinking, he wasn't much different when I came along.

On those rare occasions when Momma and I did talk, she'd tell me she came to Jesus later in life. She'd tell me she was sitting in church, about to leave, when Jesus told her that if she left, she'd die on the spot. So, she went to the altar and prayed and accepted Jesus into her heart.

Papa never struck me as someone to give those kinds of ultimatums, but I never dared tell Momma that. She'd have busted me for sure.

Momma was short like me. Daddy called her a wasp of a woman. She had a sharp tongue and always had an opinion. There was never a time she didn't think someone wanted to hear it either.

Did she love me? I think so. We went to garage sales together, we went on trips to

other states to see family, we laughed sometimes, and most of the time it was peaceful
in the house. So why didn't I miss her?

One girl I went to college with lost her
momma, and I thought the world had come
to an end for her. I had no frame of refer-
ence for what she was going through, and
every time I tried to think of something to
say, I'd fall flat. My momma was gone, and I
was just fine.

"Papa, what's wrong with me that I don't
miss my momma? Doesn't it mean something is wrong with me if I don't? Please
answer me. Please give me an answer so I
can tell Chrissy tomorrow."

The breeze picks up. It's got a sharpness
to it now, and the clouds that were rolling
in have taken over the sky. I peek out from
under the roofline and see scary-looking
clouds. We're about to have rain that blows
sideways.

I feel Papa hold me. It's a warmth that

travels over my entire body. The only answer I have to the question is that Momma and I just didn't have that kind of relationship. I don't know why. I may never know why, and it's okay. Sometimes people just don't connect.

Papa says, "Be grateful you had someone that cared for you the best they knew how."

Now, *that* I believe. Momma cared for me the best she knew how and with all she had. She wanted the best for me, and her best just wasn't my best, and that's the way it is. I left for college, got good grades, and was living a pretty happy life until I came home and knifed my daddy.

I start to think on Daddy, and Papa says I'm not ready for that yet. My heart needs some shoring up before I head into that dark tunnel.

CHAPTER SIXTEEN

The next day, my therapist appointment goes better than I expect, but I'm done before my hour is over. Chrissy sends me on my way with more homework: to think of the best time I ever had with my momma. She doesn't see me roll my eyes as I walk out the door.

Outside in the fresh air, I try to let the sun burn away what I've spent the last hour talking about. Unfortunately for me, the sun doesn't work that way, so I take myself to Kettlefish.

Fancy is standing behind the bar, drying glasses and talking to Mr. Marlin. I'm starting to wonder if he lives here. After my reaction at church, I don't want to be anywhere near him.

His eyes catch mine and send me warning signs I can't ignore. I sit as far from him as humanly possible in the small confines of the bar.

Fancy isn't a dummy, and she notices the exchange. She stops drying glasses and walks to the table in the far corner I've now claimed. "Is there something you need to tell me about Marlin?"

I drag my eyes from his direction as he puts out a cigarette, and I focus on Fancy. "Not that I can recall, but he gives me the shivers."

Fancy hooks a look over her shoulder in Marlin's direction and says, "You'd tell me if there was, though, right?"

Nodding, I respond, "Yeah, Fancy, I would."

"You want rum again?" She tips her head toward the bottle on the shelf.

I wave her off. "No. I just want a soda today."

She grunts a laugh. "You came to a bar for a soda?"

"Yeah, all those white sheep won't suffer a chance of being caught in here with all us black sheep. I can't handle them right now."

Fancy snorts and walks off. She returns with a large glass filled with fizzy soda and a thin straw. "I ran out of the big straws. Not sure if you want to use the little one, but I stuck it in there in case ya did. You want some company? I've dried about all the glass I can handle for now."

I shrug. "Sure. I got nothing pressing."

Fancy walks back to the bar and returns to the table with a glass full of what I suspect is beer from the tap. She takes a drink as she sits in the chair across from me. "So, what's on your mind, Lillian James?"

"I just came from therapy. I don't need any more thinkin'. Why don't you tell me what's on your mind?"

"Oh, Lilly, you know, there are some things a person ain't supposed to talk about."

"But I'm supposed to tell you what's on my mind?" I pull out the tiny eye-poker straw, lick the soda off, and stick it in my mouth like a toothpick.

"Seems like you're the one with all the thinkin' that needs spillin'."

I snort and then look at her, serious. "Fancy, do you remember my momma?"

"Of course I do, Lilly. I loved your momma. We was good friends."

She's right. I do remember them being good friends. How that is, I don't know, because Fancy was a good twenty or so years younger than my momma. I'd ask, but Fancy is known for being quite nasty about the age thing. If you ask her, she's always turning twenty-five.

"Could you tell me about her?"

Fancy leans back in the chair and takes a good swig of her beer. "Oh, child," she says with a whistle. "Your momma was a wild woman the first time I met her. She'd just left her first husband and rolled into town with two little boys. I babysat for her when she worked for Montgomery Ward in the town over. The boys would go to school, and I'd pick them up in the afternoon."

Fancy paused, a distant look in her eyes. "I met her momma a handful of times. She was a sweet woman. You know she's who you're named after, right?"

I nod. "Yeah, I know. From what I remember, everyone loved her."

"Oh, yeah, Lillian was a gentle, sweet woman. Everyone she met loved her. I guess your momma got her sass from somewhere further up the tree."

I roll my eyes.

"That sass right there, Lillian Louise James."

I snap my eyes to her. "Don't you use my middle name. I'll bite you!"

Fancy sits up straight in the chair, puffs out her chest, and smiles. "I'd like to see you try it, missy," she teases. "Anyway, you know she was married before your daddy, right?"

"I know she was married three times. I don't know anything about the second one."

"After she married your biological grandpa, which, by the way, he was a complete drunk. Worthless piece of a man. I met him once, and that was all I needed. Your momma left him, and she was right to do so. Drunk skunk, he was."

"What about the second fella?"

"Oh, he was a one-and-done. She married him and then met your daddy. That fella didn't stand a chance."

"How long were they married?"

"Oh, a couple months. Then your momma started seeing your daddy. She loved George. Back in the day, he was as fine-looking as a man could be. Tall, dark, dangerous, mean as a snake to anyone he didn't like."

I keep my mouth shut and my emotions from showing while she talks.

"Lula met George, and that was all she wrote. Started seeing him before she even divorced the second fella. Oh, and did she get looks, but your momma didn't care. Lula would see people giving her the eye, and she'd straighten her back and give them the eye right back."

"Sounds like Momma."

"Girl, you don't know the half of it. By

the time you came along, she'd found Jesus. Even He couldn't tame her all the way. The mouth on Lula. You're just like her. You gotta mouth too."

I pinch my lips together and squint my eyes, giving her my mean face.

She takes a drink and waves me off, laughing. "Oh, sometimes it's good to have a mouth, but back to your momma and daddy."

I nod my head.

"George ran moonshine. Did you know that?"

"No way."

"Sure'nuff, he did. He had a still in the woods north of here. Your momma begged him to stop, so he did. He'd have done anything for your momma. Well, 'sides loving those boys. He never did like boys. He'd say so too. You know he's got a son somewhere that's his, from before Lula. That boy is a lot older than you, and he lives somewhere up northeast. I never met him, and they never talked about him much."

I'm slack-jawed. "I've never heard that before."

"Lula was a jealous woman, and George was a good-looking man with an eye for the ladies. Your momma put her collar on him, and she'd yank his leash anytime his eyes got too close to someone else's fire hydrant."

"I sorta knew all that."

"Did you know she clocked someone with her purse at the Denny's in the town over one time?"

Again, my mouth drops open. "No. Way."

"Oh, honey, that woman didn't know what hit her. Your momma finds George having breakfast with her after being gone all night long. Lula walks into that Denny's, takes her purse, and just knocks the ever-livin' daylights out of her. Wouldn't have been so bad if Lula hadn't carried a .38 special in it. She flat-out coldcocked her. Your momma is so mad her whole face is lit up like a red streetlight. Lula storms out of the restaurant, and the manager comes running out after her and starts telling her she can't do that. Lula pulls that gun out and says, 'You got something to say?'"

"My momma?"

"Oh yeah, your momma. You think all that sass and attitude comes from you? Nah, honey, you come by it honestly."

"How do you know all this?"

"'Cause I was sitting at Denny's eating breakfast with my folks when she did it. I saw the whole dang thing. If I had still been babysitting, my folks would have made me quit."

"Now, *that* I would have liked to see."

"The town talked for months, but your daddy didn't go havin' breakfast with no one after that, I can tell you that. And if he did, he didn't do it where Lula knew."

"I suspect my momma knew if he did; she just toned it down."

"Hmmm, I'm don't know about that. There's only so much Jesus could do with Lula Mae James."

I sit back in my chair and think about the months before Momma died. I remember her sitting me down, telling me she had bone cancer. She was diagnosed in August, and by January, we were burying her. Right before my high school graduation. Even thinking back now, I was sad she was sick, but her not being at my graduation didn't affect me any.

A memory springs to mind of my momma and how brittle she looked. How her spirit changed in the weeks leading up to her death. "She was really different before she died. All frail and kind and sweet."

"Lilly, death is a weird thing, and when

you know it's coming for you, you change your ways real quick. Not saying Jesus didn't change her, but He sure had His work cut out for Him."

"I'm not sad she's gone."

Fancy looks at me, no expression, not even surprise. She throws back what's left of her beer and says, "I know. I've known. I saw you at the funeral. I think you were sad, but I had a feeling you weren't going to miss her. You two had a tumultuous relationship at best. Most of it being her shielding you from George."

I can't keep the dark shadow from passing across my face when she mentions my daddy. "I can't talk about him right now."

Fancy nods. "No, I'm guessin' you can't."

Kettlefish has started filling in, and Fancy looks at the clock behind the bar. The time has flown, and I've sat here most of the day, talking to Fancy about my momma. It helps that my therapy sessions don't happen until eleven each day.

My soda is watered down, and Fancy takes my glass with her when she goes.

I shuffle out. I got no desire to deal with the regular crowd.

CHAPTER SEVENTEEN

That night I'm sitting on the deck, sipping on a soda and taking in the night air, when I hear a knock on the door. It's dark enough out that I can't see more than jeans.

I holler, "Come in." I figure if someone's here to kill me, they wouldn't knock to start with.

"Hey, good-looking," Uriah says as he comes through the door.

"Yeah, I'm so hot the sun's taking notes."

Uriah laughs, and I wonder if I'll ever

get tired of it. "Well, at least you're in good spirits. How did your therapy session go?"

I shrug. "Fine, I guess. Chrissy seemed satisfied."

"I'm sorry I wasn't around today. Momma had me on the roof fixing shingles. That last bad windstorm really nailed the house."

I glance sideways at him. "I lived."

He smiles. "Yeah, but only partly."

"Shut up, Uriah," I tease.

"Can you tell me what you told Chrissy?"

Sadness settles on me. "I can, but you'll think less of me."

"No, I won't." His tone is soft. He's being sincere, but he's looking into a dark cave without really knowing what's inside. A person can be brave until the bear wakes up.

"Yeah, you will. You say you won't, but

deep down, the parts where it counts, you will."

Uriah takes a long breath and stays quiet a minute. I think he's finally going to agree with me, get up, and never come back. Instead, he says, "Lillian, I don't know how long it will take or what it will take, but I promise you I'll never think less of you."

I just nod like I accept what he's saying as gospel, but I know. I know he's only saying it 'cause he's trying to be nice. That's Uriah. He's always been like that. When we were kids, he was the kid everyone loved. He just had this way of making everyone feel special. It's why I crushed on him.

"I know what you're thinking, Lillian. I can hear your thoughts playing like cymbals, but I meant what I said."

Shrugging, I reply, "All right. So you say."

"So talk." He leans forward, elbows on his knees like I've got his rapt attention.

"I don't miss my momma. Never have, don't now, and probably never will. We just didn't have a relationship built that way, and it's just the way it is."

He sits quietly a moment. "What did Chrissy say?"

I keep my eyes straight ahead. "She said it's okay to feel like that, but not to be angry."

"She's right. Did you tell her about being kidnapped?" The tone in his voice says he's expecting me to give the right answer, and that answer is yes.

"No."

He sets his hand on his leg and twists toward me. "Why?"

Shrugging, I reply, "She didn't ask."

Shaking his head, he leans back in the chair. "Chrissy didn't know to ask. No one knew to ask."

I shrug again. "I know, but I didn't want to tell her."

"You need to. That's something important to know."

"I don't want to tell her." My agitation
level rises with every press.

"Don't you go gettin' mad at me, Lillian
James." His tone is a mixture of playful and
serious.

I'm not mad at him. I'm mad at what
happened while my momma took me. I
don't want to tell what happened, and if I
tell Chrissy I was taken, she'll ask. If she
asks, then I'll be forced to tell.

"I'm not," I say sharply.

He grunts. "Sure sounds it."

I wave him off. "Leave me alone,
Uriah."

This time he twists in his seat to stare
straight at me. "I won't."

*Papa, give me the good graces to not throw
my soda bottle at this man.*

He crosses his arms over his chest.
"What happened to you while you were

with your biological mom that's made you so defensive and mad?"

I thought Papa was the only one with sharp fingers. Uriah has touched a spot I'm not comfortable with at all. I don't want to tell. I told Momma, and she told me to never talk about it again. So I didn't. I've kept it to myself for twenty-nine years, and now I'm being asked to talk about it.

Tears spring to my eyes. I look away from Uriah 'cause I don't want to cry in front of him again. I hate crying. It makes me feel weak and exposed and useless.

Uriah whistles. "It must've been pretty bad."

"You don't know nothin'," I grumble. I'm a kicked hornet's nest now.

"I've killed four people," Uriah says softly.

I jerk my head toward him. "You said you were a chaplain."

"I was." He takes a deep breath, gets up,

and goes to the kitchen. He pulls out a soda and comes back. "I'm glad I got these, but, man, I wish I'd gotten something stronger."

He's not the only one. "I've thought the exact same thing several times."

Uriah laughs, but it's half-hearted. "You aren't the only one with secrets, you know."

"I know, but I was told to never tell my secrets."

"Your momma?" he asks. I can tell by the soft way he asks that he's genuinely curious.

I nod. "Yeah. She said to never tell anyone, and I haven't. I don't know if I can."

"How about we start small, then? How about you tell me other stuff? That way you can see if I'm good at keeping secrets." He takes another drink of his soda. "I'll tell you mine first, though. That way you have leverage."

"You don't have to do that, Uriah." I feel bad now that he's offering up secrets to trade. Just because his secrets are different don't mean they aren't as hard.

He sets the bottle on his thigh and nods. "I know, but I want to. Maybe if I tell my secrets, my shoulders won't feel so heavy."

"Okay." I stick my feet up on the railing and settle in for secrets. "I'll never tell a soul. I'll be like a bank lockbox where things come in and they never go out unless it's to the person it belongs to."

He smiles. "Deal. Okay. So, after high school, I joined the Army and went to basic training in Fort Benning in Georgia. It was nine weeks of the toughest training I had ever experienced, but I loved it."

I shoot him a smile. "I bet you did."

"Shut up, Lills, and listen," he teases. "So, I spend my nine weeks there, and that August, Iraqi forces invade Northern Iraq. I'm so young, and I think if I go over there as a chaplain, I won't have to worry about fighting and all that. I'll just stay behind the lines, content with being an ear for the infantry."

Uriah scratches the back of his head and chuckles. "I was such an idiot. Anyway, I'm stationed over there, and none of them see any real fighting the first couple of months. Most of my time is spent playing cards or listening to the men talk about how they miss home or their girlfriends, wives, and kids.

"One night, we're at the base. It's pitch-dark in that desert, and we're all sleeping when booms go off. Iraqi forces are bombing our camp, and people are running all over the place, trying to take cover. They break through, and me and my unit haven't seen any action to this point. All that training you think will prepare you for war doesn't prepare you for much at all when you're face to face with a group of people who want nothing more than to kill you."

His voice has turned raw, and I can hear

this is something he's struggled with. Of the things I wish, I wish more than anything that I could pluck that from his past, especially when his voice breaks from time to time.

"So, me and my buddies find what we think is good cover, but those Iraqi forces just keep pushing through. We got into a firefight, and me and two other guys are the only ones to walk away. I killed four men that night. I was only eighteen, and I had enough blood on my hands to fill a tub. I may not have wanted to fight, but those forces pushing through didn't care what I wanted or thought."

"Seems like you handled it pretty well." If there is such a thing as handling it well.

He shakes his head and works his jaw. "No, Lilly, I didn't. I killed people. I still see their faces sometimes when I close my eyes and try to sleep. It took a while and lots of praying."

"How long were you over there?"

"About six years. I love being in the military. I knew what I was signing up for, but knowing and *knowing* are two different things. I did two tours, and then they let me come back to the states." He finishes off his soda and sets the bottle by the leg of his chair.

"Why didn't you get out after your first time was up?"

Uriah smiles. "It was where I was supposed to be."

"Are you sure you aren't going to reenlist?" I'm more interested in the answer to this question than I want to even admit to myself.

Uriah shakes his head and looks out into the forest. "Nah, I'm done. I like being at home, letting my hair grow out, and seeing my momma."

"So you aren't leaving Foaming Springs

again?" A lump begins to form in my throat as what's coming hits me.

"No, I'm home, and this is where I'm staying."

That revelation breaks my heart. I can't stay in Foaming Springs.

When I don't respond, he asks, "You're staying after your therapy, right?" Uriah asks. The hope hanging on the words makes me ache.

"No." I don't even hesitate. I wouldn't be sitting where I am if I could leave. There's no way I can stay in Foaming Springs.

"I'm here. The town's not so bad." It almost sounds like a plea.

"I can't stay here. Ever. Once I'm free, I'm gone."

His breath catches, and I ache even more. "But, Lilly, this is home."

"Not for me it isn't. I won't stay here. My daddy lives here, I'll never be able to

grocery shop again, and, Uriah, I just can't."
The words come out in rapid fire.

He stands. It's pitch-dark now. Frogs are croaking, crickets chirping, and other various animal songs are playing. I can't see his hurt, but I feel it.

"I have to go, Lilly," he says softly, and now I hear the hurt too.

I don't say anything, but there's a part of me that wants to say, *See, I told you so.*

"I'll see you later, okay?" he says.

"Sure, Uriah, I'll see you later."

Guess he didn't need to know about my secrets after all, which is fine by me. I didn't really want to tell them anyway.

CHAPTER EIGHTEEN

The next few weeks, I go to therapy, work on Chrissy's homework assignments, and hang out in my cabin. I stay away from church, and, not surprising, I'm not invited either. I have a sneaking suspicion people are pretty happy I decided to stay home too.

My groceries are getting slim, though, and I'm feeling a little desperate when I run into Bo on a Wednesday after my therapy session. I've avoided him too, and this is my first time seeing him since Uriah left. He offers to do some shopping for me, and I thank him and Papa for the save.

Bo says he'll bring them tonight. The case he's working on is keeping him busy. Judge Kringle isn't budging on letting my car out. I'm still a flight risk. Wonder if he'd cuff my ankles if he knew how much I love walking.

I have yet to run into my daddy. I'm thankful for that too.

The only thing I'm not thankful for is Uriah's absence, which is achingly painful. I've seen neither hide nor hair of him since that night in the cabin. My "I told ya so" feels hollow now that he's gone. Guess it's just as well. Better to hurt a little now than hurt a lot later.

On my way back to the cabin, I take my time today. Instead of a straight shot, I see a path and decide I'll give it a wander. I don't know how far I walk, but I keep going until I can't see the road. The air is fresh, and the May sun is shining down on me. It's nice out here, and I continue to explore.

There's a huge tree up ahead, and the stream I've been hearing is getting louder and louder. When I get to the tree, it's sitting next to the stream like something out of a painting. I have no idea what time it is and no inclination to care, so I sit under the tree and rest. I figure I'll head back to the road in a bit. The sun is still pretty high in the sky, so I know I've got time.

A deer comes to the stream on the other side. It sees me but seems to be bright enough to know I'm not going hurt it. It takes a long, thirsty drink and then hangs out, nibbling on grass.

Between the sounds of the stream, watching the deer, and my walk, I'm more tired than I realized, and I'm out cold before I know it. I sleep more sound than I have in weeks. Maybe it was the walk or the fact that I'd left my thinking at the side of the dirt road leading to the cabin.

When I wake up, it's still light, but the sun is on its way down, and clouds have moved in, thick and black. *Boy, Texas, you sure know how to kill a party*, I think and laugh.

I might have rested well, but my back cracks and pops as I get up. Apparently, a bed made of dirt and grass and tree roots isn't the best for bones.

It must be later than I thought because I'm not even close to being back to the road, and it's getting dark enough that I can't see. Those clouds that have rolled in are hiding the sliver of a moon, and rain is starting to sprinkle. It's gotten cold too.

I rub my arms as I walk. The rain gets harder and harder. *There's no way I'm getting lost in these woods,* I tell myself as I keep trudging back the way I came. By the time I get to the road, I'm freezing. My teeth are chattering, my clothes are soaked, and I feel like I'm made of ice.

Bo's car is parked in front of the house. I can see my tiny light shining in the window. When I open the door, he's sitting on the small loveseat and jumps in surprise. I'm too frozen to laugh.

"I'll be out in a second," I stutter before disappearing into the bathroom.

I know Bo's out there waiting for me, but I don't want to leave the warmth of the shower. I'm pretty sure my core is still needing to be thawed. I do the responsible thing, though, and get out. I'm glad I left some PJs in there; otherwise, it might have been pretty embarrassing to try to get myself to the bedroom without Bo seeing me naked.

When I walk out, Bo's on the deck,

drinking what looks like a soda. "Hey," he says, "you feel better?"

"Yeah."

"Where did you go? For a second, I thought you'd skipped out."

"I went for a walk in the woods."

"Did you have fun?"

I shrug and sit down. Then I realize I'm absolutely starving. My stomach is growling, and I feel shaky. "I need to fix myself something to eat. I'll be back."

In the kitchen, I make myself a quick PB&J, grab a bottle of root beer, and take my seat. I'm halfway through the sandwich before I come up for air.

"Thank you for going shopping for me, Bo. I know you didn't have to, and you did anyway."

"Well, I haven't seen much of you these last few weeks. I wanted an excuse to come see you."

"You don't need an excuse, you know."

He smiles, and it makes me miss another smile I haven't seen in a while. "You know you can come to church. We don't bite. I had a good talk with Dad about his sermon that day. He's not going to do it again."

I snort and choke on peanut butter. My coughing spell makes my chest hurt. "Right, 'cause he's going to listen to you."

"He will, and he is. Plus, I like it when you're there." He punches me lightly in the shoulder.

I shake my head and finish my sandwich. "Why? It's not like your momma would let you hang out with me now anyway."

He shakes his head, waving me off. "Oh, Momma's just being Momma. You know how she gets."

"I know she sees you as the next judge, and that won't include me anywhere near you." I punctuate the sentence by giving him a pointed look.

"She knows you're my best friend, and that won't ever change. No matter what."

"Bo, your momma might be okay with us being friends, but you know good and well she'll never be okay with anything more than that. Which is why it's good we're both okay with it."

He turns to me, his eyebrows knitted together. "Who says I'm okay with it?"

My thoughts stop midstream. "Huh? Bo," I say, laughing, "come on. You know you are destined for great things, and that doesn't include the likes of me. Drug-addict parents, adopted, daddy-stabbin', silly ole me."

His lips pinch together, and he just stares at me for a second. "You just don't see it, do you, Lillian?"

"See what?" My voice lifts on the last word.

"It's why everyone wanted to talk to you in high school. It's the reason why if anyone had a problem, they'd come find you. It's the reason people are drawn to you. You're so down-to-earth, plain and just simply beautiful." He's talking like it's just a known fact, which is flooring me. We don't remember things the same way.

I turn to him, crossing my arms over my chest. "Bo Anderson, you've done lost your mind."

Shaking his head, he mirrors me. We're like gunfighters at high noon. "I haven't. I'm just being honest with you."

"Honest, my rear-end." Now I'm downright mad and not hiding it.

Bo's eyebrows furrow as he looks at me, and I wonder what else is about to fall out of that crazy mouth of his. He pulls out his phone and looks at it. "Okay, I'd better go. I have a continuing-education class in Austin for the next couple of days, and my flight leaves early in the morning."

"I'll be here when you get back."

Bo snickers. "I know."

"Get out, you jerk." I pop him on the thigh.

"See ya, Lills."

"Much later, Bo."

CHAPTER NINETEEN

The next time I see Chrissy, I dread what she's going to ask me. We've spent the last few weeks talking about my momma, and I let it slip at the end of our last session that I'd been kidnapped. I didn't mean for it to come flying out, but those words got wings and a mind of their own.

I'm sitting in the chair, sweating bullets, just waiting for her to pounce. "Well, aren't you going to ask? Go ahead, get it over with. Let's talk, and you can give me my homework—"

She interrupts me and says, "Stop."

I'm looking down at my hands. I'm not ashamed of being kidnapped. It's not like I had a say, but I'm ashamed of what happened while Lucy had me, and I just know it's seeping out of me like sap from a tree.

"Lilly, if you aren't ready to talk about it, I understand. I think it would be good for you to talk about it, but I'm not going to push you." Her voice is gentle and kind.

I take a deep breath. "It happened. Lucy took me. I can't change it, so why dwell on it."

"Tell me what you can, okay?"

My chest tightens, and my heart races. "All right," I say barely above a whisper. "Momma was sitting in front of her sewing machine one day. You know where it used to sit, right?"

"Yeah, I played in your house enough to remember that."

"Well, she's sitting there sewing, and Lucy comes in. They're talking, and Lucy asks if she can take me for ice cream. It's not a big deal. Lucy would still come into town from time to time to see me and take me places. She and Will, my biological daddy, had given me to Momma and Daddy, but it wasn't official yet. So, Momma says Lucy can take me."

"Okay," she whispers, never taking her eyes off me.

I lick my lips and rub my sweaty palms on my jeans. "Lucy takes me by the hand, and we walk out of the house, out of the gate, and around the corner. We're walking, and I can see a green car up the street with the back tailgate down. As I get closer, I realize it's a station wagon.

"We get to the car, and Lucy picks me up, puts me in, and jumps in the back with me. She closes the tailgate, and next thing I know, we're driving away. We drive a while, and then I start seeing planes coming and going."

I'm pretty proud of myself 'cause I'm holding it together pretty well for the moment. I smile and laugh nervously. "I don't remember a whole lot beyond this point."

"Well, just tell me what you can recall and remember, no pressure," Chrissy says.

"Okay. I remember seeing a plane and pointing at it, and the woman driving bit my finger. I found out later she was Lucy's momma. I was supposed to be named after her, but when I was born, Lucy said I didn't look like a Gertrude. I looked like a Lillian," I say and laugh.

"Momma told me Lucy took me to West Virginia. All I remember about being where I was, was that I was in an apartment. I don't know how I know that, but I do.

"Lucy had a man friend. I think they wanted to have a night alone because she locked me in her room. I found her makeup and played with it. She said I ruined it. I just remember her face being really red, and lots of angry words."

I stop talking for a moment. At this point, tears start to pool in my eyes. The next part of what happened to me is the part that's the hardest to tell, and it's the part I remember the most vividly.

I start to say something, and I catch Chrissy looking at me. My throat closes, and I pop up out of the chair to go stand at the window.

"Lilly, it's okay. You don't have to say anything. I know telling me all of this was hard. I can't imagine carrying it on your own."

"Daddy blamed Momma for Lucy taking me. Never forgave her. He didn't know what happened while I was there, and as far as I know, Momma never told him either. Daddy was mean and vengeful. I think she was afraid he'd kill Lucy. I think she was more afraid of losing him than anything," I blurt out. It's the nerves getting to me, and now I'm wondering if it was true. Maybe Momma didn't think and Daddy didn't even care. Maybe she just didn't want me talking about it.

"Well, that certainly lines up with what Fancy told you."

"Yeah."

Chrissy takes a deep breath. She wants to go on, but I can see that she's trying to think of me too. "I want to continue this later. I know our hour isn't quite over yet, but I think it's okay to call it quits early today. I do have homework, though."

"I figured." A nervous laugh pops out.

"When you come back next time, I want you to tell me what happened."

I'm out the door before she can finish the sentence. It's a painful memory, and I was told to never speak of it. I've kept it all this time. I've survived, made good grades, lived with it all this time, so why now?

Why now, Papa, why now?

I stumble out the door and straight into Uriah. He's got his hands in his pockets, and it looks like he was walking somewhere.

"Hey, Lills."

I tuck my head and keep walking. I've got nothing to say. It's been over a month since I've seen or spoken to him. For someone itching to know all my secrets, he's sure been mighty absent.

"Lills!" he yells and runs to catch me.

"I've got nothing to say to you, Uriah. I'm not planning on staying here, and you are. Find yourself a girl who's gonna stay here and marry her. I hear Misty's on the market."

He grabs me by the arm and spins me to face him. "Lilly, you stop your nonsense right now. I know I made you angry, but

I've been waiting for you to come out of your therapy session so we could talk."

"I'm going to Kettlefish. If you happen to be there, then I guess I'll see you there," I say and start walking again.

Uriah walks quietly next to me the entire way to the bar. He tries to open the door for me, but I block him. I don't want his help, and I don't want him.

It smells like beer and cigarettes and peanuts. Not a clean smell, but it's growing on me. It's become a familiar place to hide from the good people in this town. I know I'm not good people. I never did fit in.

The table I've occupied in the past is free, and I take a seat with my arms crossed in front of me. Uriah walks to the bar and strikes up a conversation with Fancy. She looks my way and smiles. They talk a while, and then Uriah comes to the table with two glasses.

"I can get my own drink when I'm ready for it," I snap.

"Lillian James." His tone is stern.

I look up at him. I hate that he's cute. I wish he looked like a clown who's been through a cheese grater. Then he smiles 'cause he can see my face soften at the thought. I don't want to make amends with him, but my whole body is saying something completely different. I feel...betrayed.

"I'm sorry, Lilly. You have every right to be mad at me. The first time you tell me something I don't like, I split, and you don't see me again for more than a month. There I was, asking you to tell me all your secrets, but I couldn't even handle something as silly as you not wanting to live here in town."

I take a big sip of my soda and just look at him. The bubbles tickle as they go down. What's there to say?

Uriah sits and takes a drink. "How you been?"

I want to say, *Like you care,* but I don't. I hold my tongue and talk to Papa instead.

Papa, please make him go away again. Make him go away and not come back this time. He deserves better. You know it. I know it. I bet his momma knows it. Why doesn't he know it? My heart hurts.

Papa says, *Be honest, Lilly.*

"You left, and you didn't come back. I didn't do and say what you wanted me to, and you left. Why didn't you just stay gone? You know you deserve better than me." I try to hide the hurt in my voice, but I can't. My heart's there, lying on the table between us, beating wildly, flayed open, and it just plain stings.

Uriah's voice catches as he starts to speak. He pins his eyes on the table, clears his throat, and starts again. "I'm sorry. I can't change what I did, but I can be different from this point forward." When he lifts his eyes to mine, I see shame. He knows he's hurt me, and right then I think he hurts worse than I do because of it. "And, Lilly, who says I deserve better than you? Who in this town is better than you?"

"Misty, Chrissy, Jenny, and everyone else. You aren't limited to Foaming Springs."

"I don't want those girls, here or anywhere else. Besides, don't you know Chrissy is getting married?"

My eyes go wide, and my mouth parts. "Nope."

His lips lift at the corners like he's thrilled he's shocked me. "She's getting married to Phillip Easterly. Remember him?"

I blink, trying to remember the name. I have a vague recollection. "Yeah, I think so."

Uriah takes a sip of his drink. "He was a

sophomore when we graduated. He runs Thriftway now."

"I had no idea."

"Jenny's married, by the way. She married some guy who works the oilfield. The reason you haven't seen him is 'cause he's in the field a lot."

"Misty's not married. There's always her."

The door opens, and Misty Morning glides in on her split hooves. "Speak of the devil."

Uriah laughs and turns around to see Misty. "Hey, Misty, why don't you join us?"

I kick Uriah under the table and whisper, "No!"

Misty smiles a wide, toothy grin. "Well, hello, Uriah, what are you doing in here?"

"Just visiting with Lilly."

"I've got to get some papers notarized. Give me just a second, and I'll sit a spell." She winks and prances over to Fancy.

Uriah turns to me. "See, she's not all bad. Just give her a chance."

I shake my head in frustration. "Whatever. Why don't you just leave me be?"

He gives me a pointed look. "You play nice, missy."

"She doesn't like me, Uriah."

His eyebrows knit together. "Maybe it's because she doesn't know you. Once she does, she'll have no choice."

I'm left speechless. He sees me in a way I'm not sure I'll ever be able to see myself. Someone worthy of affection and friendship.

CHAPTER TWENTY

In an effort to show Uriah I can be nice, I take a deep breath and prepare myself for Misty as she walks back to the table. The last thing I wanted when I walked in here was to talk to anyone. Except for maybe Fancy. Instead, I'm drinking a soda with Uriah and Misty. I like Uriah, and I don't want to talk to him, so imagine how I feel about Misty.

Misty takes the seat next to Uriah and smiles all flirty at him. "How are you today?"

"I'm good. What kinda thing were you getting notarized?"

"Oh, you know, just stuff."

"Just stuff?"

"Well, Daddy's got the idea to rename the business, so he wants to get it all done formally. I'm getting all the paperwork together for him."

"That's mighty nice of you."

Misty tosses her red hair over her shoulder and pushes her chair to where she's basically sitting across from Uriah like I'm not there. I'm already tired of her shenanigans.

I can't hold my tongue. I'm grumpy, and, well, I'm sick of Misty treating me like dirt. "Misty, why do you hate me? What did I ever do to make you be so nasty to me? Did I do something when we were kids? If I did, I'm sorry. I don't know what I could have done, but I truly, sincerely, and earnestly apologize."

I've caught her off guard. I've caught myself off guard. I had no intention of saying anything, but it just rolled off my tongue before I could stop myself.

The shock of me apologizing makes her sit back a little. "You didn't do anything to me. I just don't like your kind."

"What kind?" I ask.

"The kind you come from. My family is upstanding citizens. We work hard, go to church, marry once, and we certainly don't turn out drug addicts. I've heard Daddy and Momma talk about you since I was a kid. 'Stay away from that trash,' they'd say. You're trash. Your momma and daddy was trash, your grandparents is trash, and you is trash." Her thick Texas accent covers the entire speech. "When you left, it was the best thing to happen to this town. All we needed was that daddy of yours to go, and we'd be free of all the trash in this town."

My eyes are watering. I've done nothing

to her but be born. She hates me because I'm breathing. I'm sure I've been hated before. Maybe because I got good grades or because I said something I shouldn't have or a myriad of other reasons, but Misty Morning and her entire family hate me because of my family. I have nothing to say to combat that. I can't argue with her. If I'm honest, my family *is* trash.

"Misty..." Uriah says, his face registering a shock I've never seen.

Misty jumps. She's forgotten he's been sitting next to her. Her mouth opens to speak, and she squeaks. "I-I..." she stammers.

For a moment, she looks like a fly caught in a web, stuttering and stammering, then she gets her wits again. She straightens her back and points her nose in the air. "I'm right. She's trash. Uriah, you know she's trash. The whole church has been talking about her and her trashy family."

He stands and looks down at her hoity-toity self. "You know, I think this town has it backward when it comes to trash."

Misty pops out of the chair and flashes him a nasty look. "You mark my word, Uriah Pendleton, Lilly is nothing but trouble and trash." She flings her purse over her shoulder and prances out like she's too good to have ever been in there in the first place.

"You all right?" Uriah asks as he sits back down. "I'm sorry. I honestly thought—"

I shrug and wipe my eyes. "She's right. I am trash."

"No, not to me. Not ever."

"I wish you'd leave me alone."

"You missed me when I did."

I open my mouth to argue, but I can't. I did miss him. I missed his smile and his sweetness and his everything. His hair has even grown out enough that it's curling over his ears and floppy against his fore-head. Just like in school. Just like I like.

He leans forward with his arms on the table. "I know I missed you."

"I don't want to. I don't want to miss you. I don't want to even like you as a friend. You abandoned me, and I'm not good enough for you anyway." I swipe a tear that escapes. It's my turn to leave Kettlefish. "Don't follow me. I need to think," I say and run out of the bar.

Uriah says something, but I'm already gone.

Out of the bar, I take off for the cabin. I run and I run and I run. I find the road leading to the tree and take it just in case Uriah has decided to follow me. I need away from him and this town and all this thinking. I feel like a piece of paper being crumpled in someone's hand.

By the time I run all the way to the tree, my lungs are burning and I can't catch my breath. Putting my hand on the rough bark of the tree, I bend over, breathing hard. My hair sticks to my head because of the sweat, and my clothes feel gross. I look at the stream. The water looks cool, and I just run and jump, a split-second decision, and the water covers my head and rolls around me. The current is faster than I'd anticipated.

Pushing with all my might, my face breaks the surface, and I take a deep breath. The water carries me downstream, and I paddle fast to make it to shore where I pull myself up and drop to the ground on my stomach. I'm exhausted. I've run I don't know how many miles and then taken a dip. My own mini ironman. I laugh as I lie there.

The sun beats down on me, and it feels so good to just lie there. I'm alone for all of two seconds.

Papa.

"What do you want?"

A soft breeze tickles my skin. The water has chilled me, and I shiver a little.

"I don't want to talk right now."

Papa says, "We need to talk."

"You talk, and I'll listen. How's that for a change?"

I flop onto my back and look at the sky. White puffy clouds are sailing by in the shapes of all sorts of things. I concentrate on one that looks like a poodle.

Papa speaks softly. "Oh, my Lilly of the Valley. My sweet, sweet girl. Do you really think you're trash?"

I stay quiet.

"You are so beyond loved. I love you from the top of your head to the tips of your toes. I love when you aren't lovable or even likable. I love you so far and so deep and so wide that you cannot fathom the depth of my love for you."

"Then why let all these bad things happen to me?" I curl into a ball, and the tears pour. It's an ugly cry, and I'm glad I'm alone.

I feel Him wrap His arms around me, and I don't want His comfort, or, at least, I don't think I want it. I want to hurt like the trash that I am. I want to be ugly and disgusting and broken and angry and bitter. I want to be trash because it's easier to believe I'm trash than it is to believe I'm loved.

"Why haven't we ever talked like this before? Why now?" I ask.

The way the breeze flits across my skin tells me Papa is chuckling. "You never stopped running long enough to have a talk."

"But we've talked before."

"Superficially. The way you would with an acquaintance. I want to be more than just a passing friend. I want to be your Savior. The lover of your heart. I want you to know me so well that you see yourself the way I see you. I want you to know me so well that when you look in the mirror, you see what I see. A creation so wonderfully made and so wonderfully loved that all your cracks fade and all you see is me in you."

"I don't know if I can, Papa. How do you fix someone that doesn't know how to let anyone fix them?"

"Don't worry about being fixed."

"How? How can I not worry? Don't you expect me to be better soon?"

"Things that change quickly never stay changed. All I need is a willingness to change. A heart and ears willing to hear."

"I won't always, you know. I'm stubborn and mean—"

"Stop. Stop telling me what you think you are and listen to what I know you are. You belong to me. You are mine. Give me you and let me do the fixing."

"Okay, Papa, I'll try. That's all I've got, is try."

"We'll start with try."

I feel Papa smile in my heart. I feel His arms around me and a comfort I haven't felt in years. I know I'm still broken and that my pieces are still jagged. I know I'll still hurt before He's finished, but I know He loves me. I'll just have to remember that in the future, which may not be as easy as it is right now.

"You'll have to remind me," I say and yawn.

"I'll remind you, sweet Lilly. Don't think I won't."

I can't keep my eyes open. The day has taken all my energy, and I just can't move.

CHAPTER TWENTY-ONE

It's dark when I wake up. I sit up and look around. The moon is covered by the billowy clouds I'd seen earlier. I don't know what time it is, where I am, or how to get home. Momentarily, I'm panicked. I haven't been in these woods since I was little.

I try to remember what things looked like when I pulled myself up on the shore. Was the tree over there? I think really hard. No, it wasn't. I floated downstream. I don't even know how far, either.

I stand and try to get my bearings, as

lost as Superman in a warehouse full of telephone booths. What do I do now?

Walk. That's what I'm going to do. I'm going to walk away from the stream in a straight line and keep it to my back. It'll be quicker. I'll get to the edge of the road, and I'll be fine.

My plan starts to fall apart after a while. It makes me wish I've been using my cell phone. I haven't used it since I got to town. No point, really. The only people with the number were in Austin, and they knew I needed time. What's the point of a cell phone if no one is calling you? Only, the point is crystal-clear now that I'm lost in the woods without one.

I stop walking after my feet begin to burn. My endurance level is pretty high, so I know I've been walking for a while when I find a tree and sit with my back against it. The thought hits me that I'm in the woods and there are all kinds of creepy crawlies living here.

There's nothing I can do about my current situation, so I lean my head back against the tree and watch the sky. The clouds are broken now, so the moon shines through here and there as the wind picks up, and I can taste the dirt in my mouth. The ground is still moist from all the rain we've been getting. I wish I brought a jacket, but it was too hot when I left the house this morning.

The wind picks up again, and the trees shimmy. It's cold. You'd think by the end of May it would be livable at night, but, again, it's Texas. Nothing about the weather in Texas makes any sense to me.

The next time the wind blows, I take a deep breath. The air is chilly, but it feels so good in my lungs. I love when the air has a sharpness to it. I don't necessarily want to stay in it, but I do love it.

The woods are singing, and I relax enough that I drift off to sleep again.

Morning is tinged gray when I wake up, on my side, mouth in the dirt. I spit and sputter as I push off the ground. Stretching, I take in my surroundings, and I'm still lost. I can hear the stream, but I can't tell which direction the noise is coming from.

I'm hungry too. I didn't eat anything yesterday, and that soda is long gone. My mouth is dry, and I smack it, trying to get the juices flowing. There's no point sitting here all day, so I push off and start walking again.

I walk and I walk and I walk. When I sit the next time, the sun is high in the sky, and I can feel the burn in my cheeks. The exertion is getting to me. I've had no food or water for a good twenty-four hours, and I can't hear the stream either. Maybe I should have turned around, but by the time I realized that, it was too late, and I didn't know where to turn.

My backside starts hurting, so I figure it's time to start walking again. This time I'm less motivated to get anywhere.

Of course, that's when Uriah Pendleton comes to mind. I've known him since I can remember. The first time I saw him, I was in first grade. He was playing with Bo, Misty, and Jenny. I didn't fit in much. With my parents being older, I was used to being around older people.

I could speak granny, but I couldn't speak the language of people my age. I was always the outsider. I know Uriah and Bo think I wasn't, but they don't remember it right. The fringe is where I lived. Just on the outside of everything great.

How Bo and I became best friends, I don't know. One day we just became friends. I went over to his house, and he had matchbox cars and fire trucks, and that was it. He had fun toys, and he was now my friend. We played Batman and Robin, built indoor forts, and watched reruns of *Mork and Mindy*.

Oh, how I loved days he came over to play. Then I realize, he never came to my house to play. Never. Not once. I would play at his house, and we would have fun, but when I asked if he could come over, his momma would say no.

That thought brings me to a dead stop.

His momma and daddy think I'm trash too. Is a preacher supposed to think someone is trash? I shrug. Why not? They're people too. They can have likes, dislikes, and opinions just like the rest of us. I'm not mad at the realization. I'm not even hurt. Why, if Bo had been my baby, I may not have let him play at my house either.

I remember one time at Bo's house, his momma caught him wrestling with me. We were maybe thirteen or fourteen. She snatched him up by the ear and pulled him out of the room. I couldn't hear what was being said through the door, but I could certainly hear the anger in his momma's voice. After that, our time was spent at school, youth group, or with a crowd. I was never allowed back at his house again.

That Texas sun is draining me dry, so I start walking again. The lack of food and water take their toll on me, and the farther I walk, the more tired I get. I smell rain as the wind picks up, and it has teeth this time.

When the sun starts disappearing, I look up to find dark clouds have yet again rolled into town. The rain starts quickly. One minute it's dry, and the next, I can barely see in front of me. There's no shelter to be seen, so I just keep walking the best I can.

Stupid me. That's right; I'm stupid. I should have sat my rear-end down the moment the rain started, because I don't go six steps and I trip over something and hear a pop. When I try to stand, my ankle gives out, and it's throbbing.

Now I'm lost, wet, cold, and hurt. It's also dark, and I'm tired. I lie on the wet ground, getting beat by hard rain, and I wonder if anyone misses me. I hope Uriah or Bo does. I hope they miss me enough to look for me.

Then my doubts and fears start plaguing my mind. I told Uriah to leave me alone. I told Bo he deserved better too. They both deserve better than me. It doesn't mean I don't want to be wanted anyway. It just means I'm aware that I'm no good. Not to them. Not to anyone.

I'm not gonna cry this time. There's no point. If I die in the woods, Uriah and Bo both can move on and find someone worthy of their affection.

Papa, if I'm supposed to die out here, please

let them know I cared. I truly cared. I know I had a mouth, but I did care. It's why I said they deserve better. It's why I keep pushing them away. I'm okay with dying, Papa. I'm not mad at anyone either.

I talk to Papa until I simply can't keep my eyes open anymore.

CHAPTER TWENTY-TWO

I know when I wake up that I'm not out in the woods or in my cabin because whatever I'm lying on is soft, clean, and smells like lilacs. I'm warm too, which is why I know I'm most definitely not in the woods. I see Uriah's face looking down at me and realize I'm at his house.

Then I gather my wits, and things seem a little clearer. My throat hurts, and when I breathe, it feels like fire racing down into my lungs. I move, and it gets Uriah's attention. He's gathering me in his arms, holding me so tight I wonder if he's trying to suffocate me.

I pat him on the back and say, "It's okay. I'm okay." It comes out like a hoarse frog croak.

"Oh, my Lilly," he says. "Do you have any idea how worried I was?" It comes out as broken sobs as his lips move against my ear.

"I'm sorry," I whisper, not because I want to, but because it's the best I can manage.

He keeps me in his bear hug, like he's afraid that if he lets go, I'll disappear. "You were gone two days. It took me and Bo and several others in the town to find you. Bo's already talked to Judge Kringle."

"How much trouble am I in?" It hadn't dawned on me until right then that taking off and getting lost could get me in even more trouble. Something else hits me then too. Uriah came for me, and I bask in that knowledge. He cared enough to look.

A few seconds pass before he speaks, but I feel him swallow hard. "You're not. Chrissy stood up for you. That was before we realized you were lost. Once we figured it out, Judge Kringle was a real softy."

"How did you know I was lost?"

"I had a feeling. I just knew you wouldn't run like that. I knew you were troubled when you left Kettlefish. I came by the cabin later that day, and you were nowhere to be found."

"But how did you know where to look?"

He lets me go, resting me back on the bed, and palms the side of my face. The way he's looking at me, all worried and sweetness, like he can't believe I'm there, makes me feel gooey. "I came back to the cabin the next day, and you were still gone. As I was driving back to town, I saw the little path off to the side. I got out and followed it until I got to the stream. I just knew you'd jumped in the stream. I went back to town, got Bo, told Fancy, and people came out to help. Fancy's the one who found you."

"What day is it, and where am I?"

"It's Saturday night, and you're at my house. Even as torn up as you were, you were fighting when they started talking about taking you to the hospital. So I offered to let you stay here. Doc Stevens came here. He said your ankle is going to be okay. It was pretty swollen when we found you. You were ice-cold too."

For a moment, I stiffen. I'm in Mrs. Pendleton's house. If she thinks I'm trash too, then I don't want to be in her house. It doesn't make me mad if she thinks that way. It just makes me want to not disrespect her and to keep my landfill out of her house.

"Lilly, my momma likes you. Always has. You're welcome here, now and anytime."

I didn't have to say anything for Uriah to know exactly where my mind was going and what I needed to hear from him. What if he knew all my wickedness? How much better would his comfort be?

Then I think of Papa. That's how He knows to comfort me. He already knows all my blackness. The darkness that bleeds out the edges with hands that seem to latch on to the people around me. He still loves me. Still wants me.

"You sure?" I ask.

"I'm sure," Mrs. Pendleton says, leaning against the doorframe. She's got one hand on her hip and a hand to her throat, playing with the pendant on the necklace that's around her neck. "I'll let you know if something's bothering me, sugar."

I look at her. She's a tall, thin woman. Her face has wrinkles in all the right places and tells a story of a happy woman. She smiles, and I know I've read it right. The brightness I see in Uriah, I see in her. She loves the way he loves. That's where he got it from.

I'm humbled and thankful for the kindness she's showing me. "I don't have any better words than thank you."

A smile reaches her eyes. "I don't need any better words than thank you. You hungry?"

My stomach does the salsa, a few backflips, and then growls like a rabid dog.

"I'll take that as a yes," she says, chuckling, and pushes off the door and walks away.

Uriah continues to sit on the bed next to me. "She's going to make biscuits and gravy."

"Mmmmm…" But, honestly, leftover toe jam would taste good right about now.

"You know how to cook biscuits and gravy?" he asks.

I snort. Not hardly. "I think I'm the only

woman in the world that's managed to burn water."

He chuckles. "That is not music to a man's ear."

Narrowing my eyes, I smile. "Then perhaps that man would be better off skipping to the next song."

He mirrors my expression and leans down a fraction. "Perhaps that man should be happy with the song he's got because he's listening to a song he loves."

I narrow my eyes at him some more. "You talk like this to girls when we were in school?"

Uriah pushes my hair back from my face and traces my jaw with his fingers. "I had eyes for one girl, but she was always occupied with someone else."

If he's talking about me and Bo, he was seeing something that wasn't there. "Your eyes must not have been focused. You sure you don't need glasses?"

He shoots me a smile. "I can see just fine."

I'm too tired for all this dancing and crud. The sigh that escapes my lips describes my level of tiredness without me even speaking.

"I need to let you rest," he says and moves like he's going to stand.

I put my hand on his arm. "Uriah, please don't go."

He stops in his tracks. "I'll stay as long as you want."

The way he looks at me makes me wish with all that's in me that I wasn't so broken. I don't know if I'll ever feel good enough for him, and I don't know if I can love him the way he should be loved. I don't ever remember experiencing anything like this because there's nothing in this world I've wanted more in my life than Uriah Pendleton. It makes me hurt so deep and so pure that I can't keep myself from crying.

Uriah thinks I'm crying because I was lost in the woods. His face gets this serene look on it, and he picks up my hand. "It's okay, Lills. You've been through a lot." He wipes my tears, leans down, and kisses my forehead. I know Uriah enough to know it's nothing but kindness. "You've got nothing to worry about here. Get some rest. I'll wake you up when Momma is done with dinner."

Between my heart, Uriah, and the exhaustion I'm fighting, I can't seem to find peace. The last time Papa and I talked, I felt pretty good. I thought for sure it would stick, but I'm feeling like wax paper, with all His talking just sliding off into the waste bin.

I close my eyes and start counting, hoping it will put me to sleep. Things get really fuzzy when I hit about forty-two.

CHAPTER TWENTY-THREE

Against Uriah's protests and, to be fair, my better judgment, I stay less than a week at Uriah's house. I insist on being back at my cabin. The idea that the town lips could be flapping bad stuff about Uriah or his momma bothers me.

I've taken up my usual spot on the deck, feet on the railing, watching the woods, when there's a rap on the door, and Bo lets himself in with a yell, "Hello?"

"Hey." My voice still sounds tired even with all the resting I'm doing.

"How are you doing?" he asks as he steps onto the deck.

"I'm fine," I say and move my ankle. It still hurts pretty badly.

"You missed Wednesday night church tonight."

I take a quick glance at him. "Missed means I was aiming to be there in the first place."

"You're not going to come anymore?" he asks as he sits next to me.

"Why?" I scoff. "I can judge myself just as harshly as those church folks. I don't need a choir for backup."

"Lilly, they're just…"

"Jerks?"

He lets out an exasperated sigh. "Sinners."

I jerk my head in his direction. "You sure they know that?"

Bo laughs. "I didn't say they do."

I scoot down in the chair and lean my

head back, keeping my face forward. "Besides, your daddy and momma aren't wanting my kind in their church."

"What's that supposed to mean?" The sharp way he asks makes me think he's angry.

I set my feet on the deck and turn to him. "It means they've always thought bad of me. It's okay; I understand. But that doesn't mean I want it in my face all the time."

His lips are set in a hard line, and his eyebrows are knitted together. "No, they don't."

For the life of me, I can't understand how he can't see it. "Bo, you remember when we were kids? We would play with your cars and trucks and build forts?"

Bo furrows his brows even further. "Well, yeah."

I work hard to pose the question as

gently as I can. "You ever remember coming to my house?"

I can see him thinking. Under normal, less serious circumstances, I'd be teasing him about smoke coming out of his ears.

"Think about it, Bo. Think real hard."

Finally, he answers me. "It's just 'cause my momma was home more. I had better toys anyway."

At this point, I'm dumbfounded. "It's 'cause your momma and daddy didn't like me or my family."

Scoffing, he replies, "That's not true. Don't think like that."

Why is he fighting this so hard? I'm not mad or upset. "You remember when we were about thirteen or fourteen. Your momma caught us play wrestling? You remember her yanking you up by your ear and yelling at you?"

What I'm saying starts hitting him like I'm throwing rocks at him and his family.

I shrug. "I'm not mad, Bo. Not at them or you or anyone. I'm just saying your momma thinks you deserve better than the likes of me. I can't say I don't agree with her. You deserve better than me."

The tension is in the lines around his face and mouth. "Lilly, she's just being a mom. She's always been like that with people. She wants what every mom wants: for their kids to be happy."

Chuckling, I shake my head. "She wants you happy with someone, and that someone is not me."

"My momma doesn't get to decide who I love or spend my life with." His tone is sharper than ever.

I let out a long sigh. "Bo, n—"

He interrupts me. "No, you listen. When you went missing in the woods, I thought about how it would be if I didn't have you in my life. It broke my heart. I know we're friends. I don't want to hurt our friendship, but I can't keep this any longer. I've loved you my whole life. I loved you before I even knew what loving someone meant. Your fiery spirit, your intelligence, and your kindness. All of it. I love all of you. The parts you don't want anyone to see. The parts you think are hidden."

I stare at Bo, wide-eyed. Uriah was right. He's sweet on me, and he's been sweet on me. I've never given him any reason to think it was mutual, but here he is.

"Well, don't you feel something for me?" he asks. "All those times we would lie on the hood of the car and look at the stars and talk about life? All those times we would hang out after the youth group went home? Don't you love me too?"

I wilt inside, not understanding how he could have felt this way. We've always been friends, and that's it. "Oh, Bo, I don't. I don't feel that way for anyone."

"Uriah." Bo spits the name like it's bitter.

Turning to him, I shake my head. "I don't."

He folds his arms over his chest and lifts his chin a little. "Liar. You're a bald-faced liar. I know you feel something for Uriah. I just hoped what you felt for me was more."

I shake my head, stand, and hobble to the corner of the railing. This is not what I planned. I put my hand over my mouth and try to think of words that will comfort my best friend in the whole world. "I don't love anyone, Bo. I don't think I can. Not really love them. Not the way they deserve to be loved."

"You don't get to judge how someone else feels loved, though, Lilly." His words aren't soft or sincere, and my heart races.

I grip the railing and hang my head. "Please don't, Bo. Please don't. You're going to get mad at me, and I can't take it right now." I turn to him. "I need my best friend. I need you to be my best friend."

Bo gets up, walks over, and stands directly in front of me. "I want to be more than your best friend, Lilly. I want to be your best friend and so much more." He tries to sound tender, but there's something else there. Something in his voice I've heard before. Not from him, but from someone else. It's not what he's saying; it's behind what he's saying. That possessive tone I've heard before.

"Bo, if you really care for me like you're saying you do, then you'll love me like I'm asking. Please, just be my friend."

The corner of his mouth twitches, his forehead creases, and he reaches out and takes both my arms in his hands. "Do me one favor," he says and licks his lips. "Kiss me. Kiss me, and if you don't feel anything, then I'll accept being friends. It'll hurt like crazy because I'm crazy about you, but I'll do it."

I stare at him, wide-eyed. Kiss him? This isn't high school, and I don't want to kiss him. It didn't work even back then when we tried it. The idea turns my stomach. What do I do? Everything inside of me is screaming no, but at the same time, if I kiss him and don't feel anything, then he'll be free to find someone who does love him. Someone who will kiss him and see nothing but him when they do.

"All right, but if I don't feel anything, then you're just my friend, and you'll find a way to be okay with that, right?" Anxiety is flooding my veins. The picture of his lips on mine flashes in my mind, and all I want to do is throw up. I don't know why I'm having this reaction, but I'd almost rather die than kiss Bo.

Bo nods and smiles. Those thin lips and

that squishy smile. I close my eyes, and I can feel him close to my face.

His mouth presses against mine, and at first, it's not as bad as I pictured it. It's just me and him and high school all over again. I don't feel anything for him other than friendship.

Then the moment shifts when his tongue tries to invade my mouth. I push him back. "I'm sorry, Bo, I can't. I just can't."

He steps closer, wraps his arms around me, and looks at me hard. "You said you'd kiss me."

"But, Bo, you have to feel this isn't right. It doesn't feel right. We may love each other, but it isn't that kind of love. It's the kind of love that skips rocks, fishes together, or sits on a deck just talking. It's not the kissing kind of love."

His body is pressing hard against me. "I want you, Lilly. I've wanted you for so long." He narrows his eyes. The way he's looking at me isn't the way I want someone to look at me, especially if what they're wanting is my affection. He's a hawk, and I'm a tiny mouse.

I'm nervous now. This is a side of Bo I've never seen. I don't know how I'm going to get out of this either. My head's swimming, and the only thing I can think of is to do what I said I'd do. I'll have to bleach my mouth after, but I'll do it. "I said I'd kiss you, and I will."

He smiles a thin, hard smile like he's won something he's cheated to get. His mouth is on mine before I can even close my eyes.

I kiss him back. I kiss those nasty, squishy lips. His hands are holding me tight, and his slippery tongue is all in my mouth. Disgust splashes at my ankles, hits my waist, and by the time he's done kissing me, I'm under it, gasping for air. I don't stop kissing him until he's done with me.

I feel a deep-down dirty I haven't felt in a long time. Those memories that had been trying to scratch at my surface have broken through, and now I remember why Mr. Marlin made me feel the way he did. Men, telling me they love me, asking me what I want, and then taking from me what they want, regardless of how I feel about it.

"Did you get what you want, Bo?" Every bit of good that tried to find a way into me has been stomped out, and all that is left is black and bitter. My darkness is a mountain, and the little light that tried to shine is crushed under the weight of it.

Bo looks at me with a puzzled expression like he doesn't know what's wrong. "Lilly?"

"I don't feel anything. I don't love you like that. I will never love you like that. I don't love anyone, and I will never love anyone. All my love. All my goodness. All my lightness died tonight," I say flatly.

He stumbles back from me and says, "But…"

"You got what you wanted from me, right?"

Bo's posture softens. For a moment, he just stands there, looking at me like I've slapped him. He opens his mouth to say something and clamps it shut. His chest is heaving in and out, and I can feel he's trying to figure out if he's hurt or mad.

"I'd like to be alone now if that's all right by you."

"I…"

I walk to my chair, sit down, and put my feet on the railing. "Be a dear and shut the door on your way out."

His shoes clack on the deck, and he stops behind me.

I look at him over my shoulder. "Don't come back, Bo. You and me. Our friendship has come to an end."

Bo's shoes clack on the floor all the way to the door. It opens and clicks shut.

Papa tries to talk to me, but I tune Him out. I don't want to talk to Him now. I don't know if I'll ever be able to talk to Him again.

CHAPTER TWENTY-FOUR

I spend the next week and a half hiding in my cabin. May has turned into hot June. The deck is covered for the most part, so I sit out there, watching the birds. My groceries seem to last, but it helps when you have no appetite.

The first couple of days, Uriah comes to the cabin, trying to talk to me. I stand behind the locked door and tell him to go away.

The depth of my darkness seems to have no end, like those caves in the movies when they throw a stone and you never hear it hit bottom.

Papa keeps trying to talk to me, but I'm in no mood to listen. I desire to want to listen. I desperately want to talk to Papa, but I'm battered and bruised and broken. I think Papa has done all this stuff to me, and He's mean. He's punishing me for stabbing my daddy. I don't know why He let all the other bad stuff happen to me, but I figure I'm due bad things because I've been bad, somehow.

I think on our conversation in the woods. I try to remember He loves me, but all my hurt keeps me distant and deaf. My soul keeps crying out for my Savior, but my broken heart keeps pushing Him away. It's a war in my spirit which leaves me feeling exasperated and confused.

I called Chrissy the first few times, and she bought my excuse, but today when I call, she says she'll see me at eleven. I still can't walk on my ankle, so I call Uriah, and he gives me a ride.

As I get in the truck, he says, "I'm glad you called." He's all vibrant and light and beautiful.

"My ankle still hurts." My voice is just as flat as the night Bo came over.

Uriah glances at me. "Is that the only reason you called?"

"Yes."

"You feeling okay?" The words are dripping with concern, but I've got my umbrella up with no plans on closing it.

I cross my arms over my chest. "Yes."

"You gonna give me more than one-word answers?"

"No."

"Talk to me, Lills." It sounds like a plea, and I know those jagged pieces I've been warning him about are cutting him.

If I talk, I'm not sure what will come out of my mouth, and Uriah has been kind to me. I don't want to throw knives at him. "I don't want to talk, Uriah. I just want to go to my therapy session and come home."

"You going to talk to Chrissy?"

"No."

"She's not going to like that."

I purse my lips and look out the window. I'm done small-talking. If my ankle didn't still hurt, I'd be walking to my appointment.

Uriah goes on talking, acting like I'm not in a sour mood. "I've been helping Chrissy with her wedding."

His cheerful spirit touches my melancholy, and I wither under the exposure. After what happened with Bo, I can't seem to shake the fog that has settled in and around me. There's a war in my spirit that I don't know how to win…or if I want to win it.

"I don't need an explanation of what you do with your time. You aren't obligated to me." Not having spoken to anyone since Bo left, I realize how detached and foreign I sound to my own ears.

"I wasn't giving you an explanation because I feel obligated. I was talking to you because I haven't seen you in a while. I've missed you."

I nod and look out the window.

"Lilly, did something happen?" Uriah sounds worried.

I grunt. "Nothing that needs sharing."

Uriah stops talking after that. When he drops me off at therapy, I tell him thank you and walk to her office.

Chrissy greets me with a smile as I walk in and take my place in the chair with my hands folded in my lap. I can't fight the gloom I feel.

Chrissy sits across from me and studies me for a while. "Lilly, are you okay?"

I keep my gaze pinned on my hands in my lap. "You should call Judge Kringle and tell him I've stopped cooperating. I'm not talking anymore."

She gasps. "But you've been doing great."

I mean it to come out shaper than it does, and I look at her. "Well, I'm done."

Chrissy looks at me slack-jawed. Her face is etched with even more concern now. "No, Lilly. I won't."

That war in my spirit is waging so loud and bloody that tears are pooling in my eyes. "I deserve my punishment. I did it. People saw me do it. I stabbed my daddy in Thriftway. I don't care why I did it, and neither should anyone else."

She looks desperate now. I used to feel desperate, so I know how it feels, but I've got nothing left in me to help her. Chrissy is shell-shocked. I can tell her mind is running a mile a minute, trying to figure out what to do. How to help me.

"There's no help for girls like me,

Chrissy. I'll tell the judge you did your best. You tried with all your might, but there's just nothing to cure what I got. I'm bad, and bad girls go to jail. It's okay, Chrissy, really." I don't even try to catch the tears that fall.

Then something happens that sends an earthquake all the way to my very core. Chrissy stands, walks over, kneels down, and hugs me. Not just hugs me but holds me tight like she can feel me slipping and she's the only thing keeping me from falling off the edge.

The show of affection is more than I expected. I expected a cold, professional distance, but Chrissy is giving me something I needed and am too lost to ask for at that moment.

"Lilly, I'm so sorry for what has happened to you. I can't take back anything that's been done to you. I wish I could. Oh, you have no idea how much I wish I could. In school and youth group, you were always the one with a quick comeback, the funny girl who made everyone laugh. I was so envious of you because you had such an ease, like you didn't care who liked you or what was popular. You were comfortable being you, and it made me so envious."

"I was envious of you 'cause you were so pretty and popular. Misty hated you, and that was good enough reason to think you were wonderful," I say.

Chrissy lets me go. "Look at us. Assuming something about the other and never really finding the truth. We could've been such good friends had I been smarter."

I wipe my eyes with the back of my hand. "You wouldn't have wanted to be my friend. It's best you steer clear of me."

"When I'm no longer your doctor, we're going to be best friends, you and me. The best girlfriends either of us has ever had."

I purse my lips and try to hold back any more tears. "I can't talk to Papa right now.

I'm mad at Him, so I'm going to tell you some stuff so I won't be so mad, and maybe I can talk to Papa again. I'm desperate for Him."

"Papa?"

"Uriah thinks I'm squirrelly. I call Jesus 'Papa.' I talk to Him a lot. He sits on my deck, and we have long spells where we just visit."

Chrissy nods. Her eyes look a little glassy.

I'm not sure what comes over me, but my mouth begins to move, and before I know it, I'm telling secrets I never thought I'd tell. "Bo came to my cabin and had me kiss him. I didn't want to kiss him, but he said if I did and didn't feel anything toward him more than friendship, then he would accept that I didn't have feelings for him. He'd accept that we were just friends."

"You didn't want to kiss him." She's not asking me. It more sounds like she's trying to understand. We've all known Bo since we were kids. To hear he's done something like that is hard for a person to hear.

"I didn't want to kiss him, but I'd heard that tone before. You know the one where someone says one thing, but they mean another? The one where you know if you don't do what they say, they'll make you anyway?"

She nods. "I do." Her voice is so soft that if there was any noise in the room, I wouldn't have heard her.

"Well, that's the tone Bo had. That's the tone one of Lucy's teenage stepboys had. That's the tone Mr. Marlin had. They would say they wanted me to make the decision, but it's really them that make it. They aren't really giving me an option. They say they are, but they aren't."

Chrissy's mouth parts as her eyes go wide, and she gasps.

Words keep falling off my tongue like

I've been holding all this in just so I can pour it out here in this office. "One of Lucy's boys, he put me and him under a blanket. Did things. Lucy caught us. Washed his mouth out with soap. I always thought she had him wash the wrong part. I told Momma, and she said to never speak of it. That if I didn't speak of it, I'd forget it. I didn't forget, but any time I tried to bring it up, Momma would tell me to stop. I was living in the past, and nothing could help the past. That the best thing to do was just let it go from my memory."

"And Mr. Marlin?"

"His wife needed help from time to time. Momma would have me go over there and help her, and he'd catch me alone. Touch me. Kiss me. I don't know how many times. I'd tell my momma, but she'd just think I was telling lies. She'd bust me and tell me I shouldn't tell stories. I didn't want to go back over there, but you didn't say no to Mamma, and she wouldn't believe me."

"Mr. Marlin?" His name is spoken like a question again, but the way she says it, her world is being tilted. People she's known, the town she's lived in…she's seeing the side that went unspoken.

My mouth is opening. I know I'm saying things, but my ears turn off, so I just keep talking like I'm not really there. "One of the last times I was at his house, he caught me alone. Put his hands all over me. Down my pants. Up my shirt. I can still smell the nasty cologne he wore. The smell of cigarettes and alcohol on his breath as he shoved his tongue down my throat and felt me up." I can't stop myself from retching. Bile pours into my mouth so fast I can't stop it.

Chrissy jumps up and grabs the trash bucket. She snatches the box of tissue on the coffee table and hands it to me.

I wipe my mouth and realize I'm pouring all my secrets into the room. The black water that was inside me is now threatening to fill the room and drown me.

"And Bo? Did he…" She stops before she gets to the hard word.

"He just had me kiss him. I just don't think he would've been okay if I hadn't. I'd seen that look before. Felt that—" I retch again. This time, it's dry heaves.

She takes a deep breath as I wipe my mouth again.

"I feel black and dirty and worthless and trashy."

"Lilly, you aren't. You aren't any of those things. The people who did those things to you are black and dirty and worthless and trashy."

"Papa said the same thing, but I don't know how to stop feeling it."

Chrissy shakes her head, and her lips tremble. "I don't know either, but you and me and Papa will keep talking until we do, you hear me?"

My mouth has a mind of its own today, and I keep spilling my words all over the room. "Uriah says he loves me, but I don't know if I can love anyone, Chrissy. And Uriah, he deserves all the best things this world has to offer. He's bright and loving and...wonderful. If I were to ever love someone, it'd be him, but I can't let my darkness leak out onto him. I can't see him like that."

I don't think Chrissy knows how to respond. What's there to say? But she composes herself and looks me in the eyes. Her face is so soft and full of kindness, like Papa gets sometimes when we're talking. "Lilly, sometimes Jesus—or as you like to call Him, Papa—brings people into our lives to love us because He loves us so much. I've known Uriah as long as you have, and I can tell you without question that Uriah loves you. I think maybe you should just let Papa work on your darkness and let yourself have just a taste of something good. You may not feel like you deserve anything good, but I'm here to tell you that you do."

I roll my eyes and snort.

"I'm not saying to walk out these doors and profess your undying love to Uriah. I'm saying to do your best to keep from pushing him away. When you get in his truck, tell him you're glad he's there or you're happy he's picking you up. Something small. Something you can handle."

I bite my lip, look down at my hands, and then back at Chrissy. "I can try."

"That's all anyone can do. You are one of the strongest people I've met in a long time, Lilly. I know your try will be the hardest."

At that moment, I see Chrissy Blakely in a way I've never seen her before. I see someone I've underestimated. Someone I've mocked and hurt. My heart pounds, and I can't take back what I've thought about her. I make a promise to myself and Papa that I'll never think those things again. "Chrissy?"

"Yeah, Lilly?"

"Thank you for being my therapist."

Chrissy doesn't say a word. She pulls me out of the chair, hugs me, and whispers, "Thank you for being my patient."

CHAPTER TWENTY-FIVE

Before I leave Chrissy's office, I stop in the bathroom to splash water on my face. I don't want Uriah to see that I've been crying. As if a little water could rinse away my grief.

My mouth feels nasty, so I swish it with water. My reflection in the mirror looks like someone who's been beaten.

"You look tired," I say to myself.

"I feel tired," I respond.

I wipe my hands, gather myself together, and step out of Chrissy's office onto the sidewalk. Uriah has waited for me right out front.

Chrissy's words swirl in my mind. As I stand on the sidewalk, looking through the window at Uriah, something washes over me. I don't have a definition for it because it's something I've never felt before.

Uriah notices me and leans over to roll down the window. "Hey, Lilly, what are you doing just standing there?"

My feet start walking, and before I know it, I'm in Uriah's truck. He looks at me and grins like his favorite person in the world just got in his pickup.

I slip across the seat, coil my arms around his neck, and hold on so tight there's a good chance I'm suffocating him. "Thank you for picking me up and buying my groceries and getting me grape soda and putting up with my sharp tongue."

He slips his arms around me and holds me to him tightly, burying his face in my neck. "You're welcome, Lilly. You're welcome."

I hold on to him like my life depends on it. For some unknown reason, I just can't let go. I know people are going to stop and stare and wonder what's going on in Uriah's truck, but I just can't bring myself to care.

"Lilly, are you okay?"

"No. I'm not. I'm not okay. I haven't been okay. I don't know if I'll ever be okay. I'll never be good enough for you. I'll never be what you need." The words come out fast and furious. My voice is wavering, and my heart hurts 'cause I don't want Uriah to know all this stuff.

Uriah holds me tighter. "I'm here. I'll always be here. I don't care about good enough or any of that stuff. I've waited for you this long. I can wait as long as you need me to wait."

I push back until I'm looking him in the

eyes. "I'm trouble. You know that, right?"

He smiles his warm toothy smile. The one that makes me feel so smooshy. "I can handle it."

"Are you hungry?"

The midday sun is bouncing off the hood of the truck, making his eyes sparkle more than ever before. "I thought you'd never ask. You want to go somewhere in town?"

"Would you go grocery shopping for me, and we'll eat back at the cabin?"

Uriah nods and gets a mischievous look in his eyes. "You gonna burn me some water?"

"I'm gonna fix you the best PB&J you've ever eaten." I smile and wiggle my eyebrows.

It sends him into a fit of laughter. He throws his head back, pulls me to him, and hugs me like the world doesn't exist.

When he lets me go, he keeps me in the

seat right next to him. I like the feel of being wanted. It's a new feeling, and one I could get used to real quick.

I sit in the truck at the grocery store. Not enough time has passed that I feel like I can go in there yet. While I sit in the truck, I watch as people come and go.

I have my feet on the dash, doing my people watching, when my day goes south. My daddy is at Thriftway, and for a moment, I think he hasn't seen me, but he has. His eyes lock with mine, and my heart races. I can't breathe, I can't move, and I can't think.

I can't even talk *about* him, so talking *to* him is out of the question, but I don't think he understands that because when he sees me, he starts in my direction. I fumble for the lock on the door and then reach over and lock the driver's door. The windows are up, and it's a million degrees outside. Good thing the air conditioning works, because there is no way I'm rolling down the windows.

Daddy makes it to the truck in record time. His eyes peer through the window at me before he jiggles the door handle and then pounds on the window so hard I think it's going to bust. "Come out of there Lillian Louise James. Come out now!"

I'm surprised he's being so loud and all, what with people being around. He's always been good about keeping this side of himself from being known, but I can see his bloodshot eyes and can almost smell the alcohol on his breath.

I shake my head.

"You come out of there right now. Just 'cause I didn't press charges don't mean you don't need a good old-fashioned butt-whoopin'!"

"No. I'm not coming out," I yell back.

"Girl," he starts unbuckling his belt and

pulls it off, "when I get a hold of you, you're gonna wish your momma was still alive."

My daddy is in his late seventies, but you wouldn't know it with the way he carries on. I'm still scared of him to this day. It's why I haven't been home in so many years. He hasn't even known where I've lived because I'm afraid of him. I came home to visit because I thought I could manage being around him just a couple of days.

My head is swimming. I'm gulping air because I feel like I'm being strangled.

Daddy pounds on the window harder and yells louder. People are starting to stand around and stare. I'm so embarrassed, but there's not a thing I can do.

"You just wait, Lillian. The next time I catch you, you won't be able to get away from me, and I'll show you. I'll show you just what I do to little girls who hurt me. I'll show you; you can bet on that!" He keeps yelling and pounding.

I put my hands up to my ears and close my eyes. "Please, Papa, please come rescue me."

"You get away from my truck!" I hear Uriah's loud military voice.

I look to see what's happening. My daddy's back is to the truck.

"You can't tell me what to do, son," my daddy smarts back. "That's my youngin' in that truck, and she's due a whoppin'."

"That's my truck, and she's my girl, and you'll leave them both alone, or you'll deal with me." Uriah isn't taking any garbage from my daddy.

My daddy mumbles something I can't make out, but he leaves.

Uriah waits until he's gone into the store, and then I unlock the door. Uriah reaches in and grabs me, and I wrap my arms around his neck. The sobs that slip out come from a place I thought I'd escaped a long time ago.

"It's okay, Lilly. I'm here," he says, his voice soothing and kind. He rubs his hand up and down my back, trying to reassure me, but I know my daddy isn't going to let this go. He'll be sure to make good on his threats.

"Y'all go home," Uriah says to the rubberneckers as they pass by.

My face is hidden in his chest, so I can't see who he's talking to. I don't care just as long as they go.

What floats to my mind next shatters me to pieces.

Daddy will hurt Uriah.

Either he'll hurt him physically, or he'll use me to do it. Most people in this town see a sweet old man. They don't know what he's like when the doors shut. They don't know his mean streak, but I do. I was the subject of it from the time I was about seven to the time I left for college.

Daddy loved me until I learned to talk. Then he didn't love me so much anymore because he said my mouth was too big for my britches. I can't count the number of times my momma took a lashing from my daddy because she stood between us. She wasn't always home, either, and when she wasn't, he'd take advantage of it. All the things I'd done that he didn't like...

I shiver just thinking about it.

Uriah lets me go and holds my face, looking me over. "Are you okay?"

I shrug. "Fine as I can be, I guess."

"I'll call Bo. Maybe he can get Judge Kringle to give you a little wiggling room, and we can go to the next town over so you can have a break."

I close my eyes and purse my lips.

"What?" he asks.

"Don't call Bo. We aren't friends anymore."

I can't look at Uriah. I can't face him and tell him what I did. He'll never look at me the same. He'll see I'm dirty and worthless.

"Why? What happened?"

I frown and cast my eyes to the pavement. "Please don't make me tell."

Uriah tips my chin up and makes me look him in the eyes. "I've been easy up to this point, but I want to know what happened, Lilly. You and Bo have been best friends for years, so something pretty bad had to have happened."

Oh, Papa, what am I to do?

The day has been hot and stale, but right then, a warm wind picks up and tosses my hair like a flag in a tornado.

It's Papa. I can feel it in my heart that He wants me to tell. My choices are pretty clear. Either be obedient or don't.

"Can I tell you at home?"

Uriah looks around. He's forgotten we're standing in the parking lot of Thrift-way. We don't have any onlookers anymore, but I still don't want to talk here. If my daddy comes back out, he'll make another scene.

"Get in the truck and lock the doors. I'm going back in to get the groceries. If he comes back, you honk the horn like crazy, and I'll be right here. You got it?"

"Okay," I say and hop back in the truck. I lock the doors and watch as Uriah marches back into the grocery store like a man on a mission.

CHAPTER TWENTY-SIX

I'm fixing my best PB&J as Uriah sits out on the deck waiting for me. I take my time because I know when I get out there, he and Papa both are waiting for me to tell him what happened with Bo. I said I'd tell, though, so, I will. I'm dirty, but I'm no dirty liar.

"You need to stop your stalling and get out here and talk to me," Uriah calls from the deck. He's caught on to my game.

I pep up my speed and walk out onto the deck with the sandwiches. Uriah got the drinks before I started making the sand-wiches. I hand him his plate and sit down with mine.

He holds it in his lap and just looks at me as I stare forward. "You're stalling, Lillian James."

I quickly glance at him. "I know." It comes out just above a whisper.

"So, tell me," he says and takes a bite of sandwich.

"That first day back in the cabin after I stayed with you and your momma, Bo came over. At first, it was a normal visit with him, but he started talking about having feelings for me and saying how he worried when I was lost in the woods and how his heart would break if he lost me."

"Okay, doesn't sound so bad yet."

I set my plate on the deck. My hunger seems to have vanished, and my stomach is in knots. "I tried to tell him his momma wouldn't have none of that. I wasn't good enough and he deserved better, but it was like he just wasn't hearing me."

"I knew he was sweet on you."

"That's not sweetness, Uriah."

He looks at me, narrows his eyes, and frowns.

"I told him I just wanted to be friends. That I didn't love him like that. I told him I didn't love anyone. Bo talked about how we would talk and watch the stars at night and hang out. He asked if I felt something for him."

"You don't feel like that about him?"

"No," I spit. "I never have. And even if I did, I wouldn't anymore."

Uriah knits his eyebrows together and gives me a menacing look. "Keep talking."

"I told him I didn't. He called me a liar when I told him I don't feel like that for no one." I look to the corner of the deck. "I got up and stood over there, and he followed me."

I've been fine telling what happened to this point, but now my heart starts racing. This is the part when I broke that night, and reliving it is painful.

"Lilly, I know it's hard for you to tell stuff, but you need to tell me. I need to know what happened." Uriah's voice is stern, but it's the kind of stern that heroes use when they're about to go after the bad guy.

"Bo wanted me to kiss him. He said if I kissed him and all I felt was friendship after that, he'd let it be. I didn't want to kiss Bo at all. The thought made me feel sick even. I've never felt like that about him, and I never will." The same urge to vomit comes over me as the memory floods my mind.

"I tried to tell him, but he just couldn't or wouldn't hear me. So, he put his mouth on me, and at first it was okay, but then he tried to kiss me like I was his girlfriend.

When I pushed him back, the look on his face…" The words die on my tongue.

Uriah growls a reply, "*What* did he do, Lilly?"

For a second, I hesitate, but I told Uriah I'd tell him, so I will. "He grabbed my arms, and the look on his face…I don't know, but I'd never seen him like that before. So I told him, 'Fine, I'll kiss you like I said I would.' I kissed him until he stopped kissing me."

"Did he force you to do anything else?" Uriah's posture softens just a fraction. His tone says it wasn't right to do any of it, but he's not looking to put Bo in a coffin.

"No, but I can tell you right now that I've seen that look before. Heard that tone of voice. If I hadn't kissed him, I don't know what he would have done. He was just like Marlin. Just like that boy at Lucy's house." I gasp as I realize I've spilled something I hadn't planned on spilling.

"Marlin?" Uriah's voice rises.

I grimace. Telling him about Bo was hard enough. "I didn't mean for that to come out. Just forget about it. I've talked to Chrissy. She knows."

"Is that stuff you told her today?"

I nod.

Uriah jumps up, hands on his hips, and looks down at me. "I'll kill both of them if they ever so much as look at you again."

I looked up at him. "You can't change what happened. Just like I can't."

"But Bo didn't do anything, right? You'd tell me if he did." Uriah has locked eyes with me. I'm not his property. He doesn't possess me. It's not ownership speaking; it's affection. The desire to shield and fight for someone he cares for.

"He did exactly what I just told you. He left that night. I told him we weren't friends anymore."

He crosses his arms over his chest,

seeming to be satisfied by my response. "But Marlin? What did he do?"

Well, Papa, if I'm spilling my beans, might as well spill 'em all, right?

"He'd catch me alone when I was over at his house helping his wife. He'd touch me and kiss me and feel me up. The last time he caught me, it went further, but not a whole lot."

"And Lucy's stepson?"

I nod. "She caught us before it went too far." That doesn't change how dirty it makes me feel.

Uriah sits down with a thud. The look on his face is something between anger and disbelief. "You've kept these secrets this whole time?"

I shrug. "I told Momma, but she called me a liar and busted me. Told me not to go spreading lies about people."

"Your momma didn't believe you?" The

way his mouth drops open, he can't fathom the notion.

"Oh, I think she believed me. I just think she didn't want Daddy being sent to jail for killing him for touching something that was his. I've realized she loved Daddy a whole lot more than she loved me."

Uriah rakes a hand through his hair. He's cut it since the last time I saw him, but it's still long like I like. "I can't believe you've gone through all of this by yourself."

"I've had Papa, but He was the only one who knew besides Momma until I told you and Chrissy. Bo doesn't even know."

Uriah stands and pulls me into a bear hug. He buries his face in my neck, and his lips move against my skin. "As long as I live, and if I can help it, not another single person will ever lay a finger on you again unless you want them to."

I snuggle into his arms and feel so warm and so protected. It's an entirely new experience for me. I've been on my own for so long that it feels foreign to have all these feelings all at once.

Then I remember my daddy, and those safe arms feel more like a lead coffin. "My daddy will hurt you, Uriah." I pull away from him.

"What makes you say that?"

"'Cause I know him. He's vindictive, mean, and horrible. He'll kill you if he gets the chance, or he'll kill me so it'll hurt you if he thinks that'll be worse."

"Then you're coming and staying at the house with me and Momma."

I shake my head. "No. I won't do that. The lips in town will flap, and all their judgment will come at you and her."

"I don't care. She won't care. I'm not leaving you if you think he's capable of that."

I realize now that I should've kept my

mouth shut. I shouldn't have told him my daddy is dangerous.

Papa, you've got to help me figure out how to keep him safe.

My posture softens, and I relax my face and try to put him at ease. "What do I know? I've been gone all these years. I stayed at the house, and things were fine until the grocery store."

Uriah's eyebrows furrow. "Do you know why you stabbed him now?"

Shaking my head, I reply, "No, I don't. I can't fathom why I'd do such a thing." I can't either. That moment seems to be locked with a key that I don't have yet.

"What I saw today makes me not want to leave you here." He takes my face in his hands, and all I can see when he's looking at me is concern.

"I'll be fine. Daddy doesn't know I'm here." At least, I don't think so.

Uriah looks at me like he's got a war inside going on. "I don't like it. I don't like leaving you alone out here."

"You've *been* leaving me alone out here, and I've been just fine up to this point."

He eyes me.

"Okay, so one time with Bo. One time I'm not so fine, but all the others I was fine."

Uriah pulls me into another hug, and we stand on the deck, watching the birds and woods until it's too dark to see.

That's when it hits me. An emotion I never thought I'd feel for someone. I love Uriah. I've loved him for as long as I can remember, and now I know why: he's never wanted anything from me but me and what I was willing to give him.

CHAPTER TWENTY-SEVEN

Mid-June turns to mid-July, and I don't see my daddy again. It doesn't really surprise me, though, 'cause I didn't see him before the time in the parking lot, so who knows where he's been keeping himself or with whom.

I see Bo every so often and shy away from him.

Uriah and I spend time together. I go to church with him from time to time, but he doesn't push me to go. When I say no, he listens and lets it go. He and Papa are working on my trust.

My therapy sessions get easier. I still don't know why I stabbed my daddy, but the other things that were weighing me down seem to get lighter the more I see Chrissy. It's not like what I thought it would be at all.

Between my talks with Papa and Chrissy, all those years of feeling like I was dirt start to get better. I won't say they're gone, but I can say better. Chrissy says I'll probably struggle with them for a while. Not because Papa can't heal me, but because it can be hard to not hurt from stuff like that.

One day, I'm in her office, and we're talking about why things take so long to heal. I'm sitting in my chair, she's sitting in her chair, and Papa is taking up the rest of the room. I know because I can feel Him all over.

"You think miracles still happen, Chrissy?" I ask.

"I think so. There are stories all the time about people being healed from cancer or other life-threatening things."

"You think Papa can heal me and make all my hurts go away?"

Chrissy's eyebrows draw together, and she thinks for a moment. "I think He can. Now, whether He will or if you will let Him is a different story. I think it's easier to heal physical stuff than it is to heal emotional and spiritual stuff because the outside stuff you can see. You know it's healed, but the stuff on the inside is harder to see and easier to be brought up again and again."

I ponder what she says for a moment. Deep stuff is hidden, which means the healing can take longer. "I can see that."

She tilts her head. "What made you think of that?"

With a shrug, I say, "I don't know. I just

don't want to have all this in me anymore. I don't want to be able to remember all this stuff. I don't want to feel it anymore."

Chrissy lets out a long sigh. "I know. I wish I could do something more to help, but I know talking about it and keeping it under a light will help."

"I'm feeling better, lighter. I think keeping it to myself let it fester and turn into a monster."

She chuckles. "Well, that's true. Have you spoken to Bo since that night?"

I shake my head. "No. I don't have anything to say."

A few seconds pass, and then she says, "Maybe he has something to say. Maybe he'll apologize. Not that it makes right what he did, but maybe it will help him be a better person."

"I guess."

"Have you forgiven him?"

That's a big question. "Papa and I have

been having a tug-of-war about that. I don't want to forgive him because I think it will make what he did seem okay, and it's not."

"Why do you think that?"

"Because if he apologizes, then he'll think things are okay and we can be friends again."

"Maybe he could apologize, and you can tell him you forgive him but that just because you're forgiving him doesn't mean what he did was okay. You can tell him you can't be friends with him anymore because you don't trust him."

I throw my hands up. "There you go, being all logical like Papa."

Chrissy smiles and laughs. "Lilly, you have the best humor of anyone I've ever known."

"Papa laughs too. I think both of you are crazy most of the time." I don't like compliments. They make me feel weird.

Tilting her head, she blinks like I've said

something foreign. "How do you do that?"

"How do I do what?"

"How do you talk about Him like that? Like He's here in the room? Like He's so real?" The ragged tone of her voice catches me off guard. She's looking for answers from me, and I'm not understanding what she's asking.

I shrug. "He is real. He is here in the room. He's Papa."

Her shoulders sag. "But how did you get a relationship with Him like that? I go to church every Sunday and every Wednesday, and I find myself insanely envious of you when you talk about Him because I want a relationship like what you have."

I think my therapy session just went haywire.

"Chrissy, it's all I had. I didn't have anyone else. I ran from here at seventeen. You and Uriah and everyone had relationships with each other. I had Bo at the time, but he never knew all the things that happened to me. I was alone all the time. I always felt like an outcast. You guys remember things way different than I do."

"But this relationship you have. It's so… tangible. I want that."

"Then have it."

Chrissy looks at me funny. "But how? How did you do it?" Her voice is so earnest…and desperate.

"I clung to the only thing I could. I have a few business associates, but I don't have any friends. He's all I had. He's all I've ever had. Momma and Daddy only let me do youth-group stuff, and anything else was strict. I didn't get to stay out or play or do anything like you and everyone else, so my only friend was Papa."

"Tell me what I can do to have what you have."

"Just talk to Him like you would your friends or your new husband. When it's just you and Him. Just talk. Ask Him to sit a spell, and then just listen to what He has to say. Sometimes it's hard to listen 'cause you got so much going on and you think He's there to just listen to you, but He's not. Sometimes He's got stuff to say, so you have to be quiet."

"Do you think if your life had been easy that your relationship with Papa would be what it is?"

Maybe my therapy session hasn't gone as haywire as I think. I take a long breath and ponder a moment. "I don't know. Maybe. Maybe not. I guess I'll never know. I wish it could've been the way it is without all the junk I've dealt with, but I can't change anything."

Chrissy smiles sly. "I'm not saying Papa caused all your mayhem, but maybe He's using it for something awesome."

"He's said that too. Still don't mean I have to like it." If I'm honest with myself, I've let Papa know it too. Since that day I hugged Uriah, I've been doing most of the talking. Oh, I've felt Papa, but He's been quiet, like He's waiting for something.

She laughs. "No, you don't have to like it. Maybe you could talk to Papa some more about letting go and forgiving these people who have wronged you. Not because letting it go or forgiving them makes it right, but because letting it go sets you free."

Grumbling, I shake my head. "You and Papa talk a lot of junk."

Chrissy snorts and chokes. When she gets her wind back, she says, "I'll be glad when you aren't my patient. I'm serious, though. Let them go." She pauses for a moment. "You want to forget. To let this stuff go and be healed. I think forgiving them will set you free to do just that. I think Papa is right. Maybe you just wash your hands of those memories, and next thing you know, you'll be wondering why you hung on to them for so long."

I shake my head and look away. "I know in my head that you and Papa are right, but it's hard to let it go. I've held on to it for so long. I didn't realize until just now, talking with you, just how hard I've clung to it. It's part of what makes me, me. I feel like if I let it go, then I'm letting part of myself go. What if I can't let it go?"

Taking a deep breath, Chrissy nods. "You might have to let it go a myriad of times before it's finally gone, but you keep letting it go so you can remain free."

"But how do I do it?" I don't hide my desperation. I want this stuff gone, but it clings to me.

"Let Papa tell you who to forgive first. Let Him guide you. That way you're doing what He wants."

I swallow hard. "You two are asking a mighty tall order, ya know?"

"I know, but we both love you and want you to be free." Chrissy looks at the clock. "Time goes so fast when you're in here."

I pop out of the chair. "Says you."

Chrissy walks me to the door. "I'll see you next time, okay? Maybe we can start figuring out why you stabbed your daddy."

My heart sinks, and I think she feels the shift in the mood.

Chrissy holds up a hand. "We've already talked about some pretty rough things. That should be a cakewalk."

"What kinda cake you been eating?"

She bear-hugs me. "I love you, Lilly."

"Thanks, Chrissy." I turn to walk, and I stop. "Chrissy?"

"Yeah?"

For a second, I hesitate. "You like being married?"

Her eyebrows rise.

I shake my head and wave off whatever thoughts she might be having. "No, don't you go thinking anything. I'm just wondering. You being married and all, I was just wondering if it's what you thought it'd be."

Chrissy smiles wide. "Yeah, Lilly, it is."

CHAPTER TWENTY-EIGHT

Uriah and I sit in Tish's Tacos after my therapy session. My ankle is all better, but I like him picking me up. Plus, it's July in Texas. As hot as it is, you'd think Satan is sitting on the state line with his pitchfork.

We're munching on tacos when Uriah looks up, and his face is masked in anger. I turn around and see Bo standing just inside the door.

And sure enough, Papa shows up too.

Uriah starts to stand, and I put a hand on his arm. "Don't."

He looks at me and purses his lips like I'm asking a tall order.

"Give me a minute, okay?"

I get up and go over to Bo. He won't look me in the eye. "Hey, Bo."

He won't talk to me either.

"I'm not mad at you anymore. I forgive you. I'm not saying we can be friends just yet, but I forgive you." I turn, walk back to Uriah, and sit down.

"What did you say to him?" Uriah asks.

"I told him I wasn't mad anymore and that I forgive him."

"I don't know how you can do that. I don't know if I can."

"Papa says we gotta. It's the only way to be free. I don't know how long I'll have to keep reminding myself that I'm not mad at him or that I forgive him. I just know I will until all the hurt is gone."

"All right. You're the boss. I'll try to do it too."

Bo goes to the counter, orders his food, and I see them hand him a bag. He hangs his head as he walks to the door and leaves without even casting a glance in my direction.

Sighing, I say, "I know what shame feels like."

"Well, he deserves that shame," Uriah replies.

"Maybe. Maybe he just didn't think about what he was doing when he was doing it, and now that he's had time, he regrets it."

Uriah chews on that a moment. "I hope so. I hope he's able to think about what he did and learn to never do it again to anyone else."

"Me too. I guess if he has to make a mistake, it's better it was done to me than someone else who would never forgive him."

He smiles at me and lets out a long

breath. "Life's going to be an adventure as long as you're with me."

"Don't go getting all sappy. I'm still broken. I'm still jagged."

"Yeah, I know, but every day you're a little less so." He winks.

I huff and roll my eyes. "What do you know?" I'm not angry or upset. Most of the time, I just don't know what to say when he tells me things like that.

He shoots me a wide smile. "I know. I see it."

"You done eating? I'm ready to go." More than anything, I want the butterflies in my stomach to stop. They seem to flit and flutter the more time I spend with Uriah.

Scoffing, Uriah replies, "You can't be done eating. You've had hardly anything."

"I've had a taco."

"One taco. Did you eat breakfast?"

"No."

"Then you need to eat more." He sets a wrapped taco in front of me.

I put it back on the tray. "I'm not hungry anymore."

He looks at me and rolls his eyes. "What did you and Chrissy talk about today?" He changes the subject and starts chowing down on his taco again.

Uriah and I have started talking about my therapy sessions. After I told him what happened with Bo and Marlin, it just didn't seem like all that big a deal anymore.

"We talked about miracles and Papa."

"Miracles?" He sets his taco down.

I shrug. "I mostly wanted to know if she ever thought I'd be free of all these thoughts and feelings, because I think it'd take a miracle."

"What did she say?"

"She said I needed to forgive so I can be free. I just have a hard time with it. That's all. Me and Papa have been talking, and

He's said the same thing. I just don't know if I can, ya know?"

He picks his taco back up. "You told Bo you forgive him."

I bark a laugh. "Yeah, 'cause I felt like I was supposed to, not 'cause I wanted to."

"Do you feel better since you talked to him?" He takes a bite while giving me a second to answer.

"I don't know how I feel, to be completely honest. All this dredging up the past, talking about things that can't change, and dealing with all this touchy-feely stuff has me confused and worn out."

"You seem to be doing better. Like I said, you seem less broken every day." He wipes his hands and then adds, "Not that I thought you were broken to start with. I'm just using your words."

I sit for a moment and take time to ponder what he's just said. "I think darkness has a way of seeping in, and it doesn't like leaving. I think it makes you feel broken, and it takes that broken and uses it as a cage. It's hard to break free from a cage that's been built for years. It's not something you just get over."

Uriah's eyes shine when he looks at me. "You always had a way with words, Lillian James."

"Naw, I'm just talking."

"Keep going. I like your talking."

I bite my lip and smile. I can't help but smile at Uriah. Spending so much time with him lately has given me a new appreciation for him and his spirit. He's more kind and loving than I ever knew. If I'd known then what I know now, I may have never left Foaming Springs.

"Chrissy said she wants a relationship with Papa like I have. I don't understand what she means, though. I mean, I just talk, and Papa is there. That's all I know."

He grunts. "I don't know about Chrissy,

but I can tell you I sometimes feel the same way."

I blink, not understanding. "What way?"

Leaning forward, his gaze catches mine. "I want to talk to Jesus like you do. I want the relationship you have. The way you talk about it makes it so familiar. It's like a married couple."

For the life of me, I can't fathom Uriah not already having that. He's kind and sweet and generous. "You can. Just talk. Or listen. I don't know what else to say. A relationship is personal. Not everyone needs Papa like I need him. He's all I had for so long that it's hard to talk to regular folk sometimes."

"Maybe if I hang out with you for a few years, I'll figure out how to have a friendship with Him like that."

"A few years, huh?" A smile breaks out on my lips, and my cheeks warm.

"Maybe more." He winks at me and

smiles a smile that melts me in places I didn't know I had.

"Stop it."

"You going to church with me tonight? It's Wednesday potluck night."

I raise my eyebrows. "I haven't been to a potluck since I first came back to town."

"There could be pie."

"You think my daddy will be there? I've heard he's coming to church more."

"I tell you what. We'll go, and if he's there, I'll take you home and we'll sit with Papa on the deck, eating PB&J's."

I grin from ear to ear.

Oh, Papa, I know I don't deserve him, but thank you so much for him.

There's a part of me deep down still waiting to lose him, but, for now, I'm enjoying the dickens out of Uriah Pendleton's company.

CHAPTER TWENTY-NINE

Papa loves me. I know because my daddy isn't at church tonight, and there's a pecan pie looking at me with love in its eyes. People are filing in, and the older women are running around in the kitchen, getting things ready. Mrs. Pendleton sees me and flashes me a big grin.

When Pastor Jeffrey walks in, he sees Uriah and starts our direction, until he sees me. It's the first time I've been with Uriah that the pastor didn't see me with him at first, and now Uriah sees with his own eyes what I've been telling him all along.

Uriah's face goes from happy to sad to angry in the blink of an eye.

"Don't," I whisper to him. "Don't be angry or sad. It's okay. I'm just not their kind."

He looks down at me and gives me the most loving look. It breaks my heart for him to have to be hurt by people. "They're no better than you," he says and touches my face with the palm of his hand. "You're better than all these people who look down at you. You have a light and a goodness they can't fathom. If they could open their minds a minute and see you the way I see you, it would change their lives."

"Uriah, I don't care what they think of me. I care what they think of you. I don't want them to think less of you because of me."

"I don't care what they think of me, so

don't you either." He puts his arm around my shoulders and pulls me in close. "Let them think what they want. It's them losing out on knowing you."

Chrissy walks in and sees me. We have to keep our distance to a degree. With her being my therapist, she doesn't want anyone to think we aren't doing what we're supposed to be doing in my therapy sessions. She comes walking over to me, smiling. "I haven't seen you on a Wednesday in a long time."

"I was here for the potluck when I first got here. I'm just not much of a churchgoer."

"I told her there would be pie," Uriah says, poking fun at me.

"Well, that's a good enough reason for me. Which one looks good?"

I point to the table. "If that pecan pie is made by the same person as the last one I ate, then it's heaven in your mouth."

Uriah bobs his head up and down. "She's right. That's good pie."

Chrissy snickers, pats me on the arm, and then walks off to stand next to her husband.

The place is full now, and Pastor Jeffrey asks everyone to quiet down and bow their heads as he offers up grace.

I peek at one point and see Bo standing in the corner, staring me right in the eyes. The look on his face is murderous. I guess he's decided he's mad about what happened, and the fact that I offered forgiveness makes it even worse.

It's not raining today, so as Uriah and I move through the line, I ask if we can sit outside and eat where it's more peaceful. He agrees, and we get our plates, pie, and drinks and find a spot on the steps away from everyone.

"Bo was giving you a pretty dirty look

during the prayer," Uriah says as we sit eating.

"You were supposed to have your eyes closed for the blessing."

"So you didn't see it?"

"Yeah, I saw it."

"Weren't your eyes supposed to be closed too?"

"I'm bad, remember?"

Uriah rolls his eyes and smiles. "I'm not comfortable with you staying by yourself in the cabin with him giving you looks like that."

"I'll be fine, Uriah. You thought my daddy was gonna get me, and he hasn't. Neither will Bo. He wants to be a judge. Can't be a judge if you commit crimes."

"His momma wants him to be a judge. Bo wants you."

"Bo *doesn't* want me. He wants me to want him, and he'll never have that. So he can be all angry and stuff if he wants to, but

I've never wanted him like that, and he knows it."

"Doesn't matter if he knows it or not, he still wants you."

"Aw, he'll get over it after a while and find someone, and then I'll just be a bad memory."

After that, Uriah lets it go and changes the subject. "You wanna take a walk down by the fishing pond after church tonight? I'll stop at the ice cream place on the way if you want."

"Sure, I'd like that. I don't know if I'm gonna want ice cream after all this, but I'd like to walk with you."

Uriah flashes a smile and pops a bite in his mouth. "One of these days, you're gonna be mine for real and forever."

"Oh, hush. You don't want me either."

He gives me a serious look I've never seen before. "That's not true. I do want you. I've always wanted you, and I want you for now and forever. But I will never make you do anything you don't want. I'll never make you make a choice or force you into anything."

"You'll get real tired of waiting and move on."

"Never. Never in a million years, Lillian James. Never in a million years."

I feel the weight of what he's saying so heavy in the air that it's hard to breathe. Uriah cares for me, and it's the kind of care that's patient and kind and loving. It's the kind of care I've longed for my entire life. The kind of care I wouldn't want from anyone else but Uriah.

Papa comes floating in like a matchmaker. I hear Him in my head and feel Him in my heart. I know I've found someone I might be able to say *I love you* to someday. If I can ever be free enough to feel that way.

Uriah locks eyes with me, and I know he's meant every word he's said. The tension between us is like a stoked fire. It's something I've never felt before in my life. I crushed on Uriah in school, but it was from afar. The time we've spent together the last few months has been more than I ever bargained for and more than I ever thought possible.

I break the silence and say, "I don't know if I can give you what you need, Uriah."

"Don't worry about it right now," he says and shrugs. "We'll cross that bridge when we come to it. I'm just letting you know what you mean to me. I want you to know that I love you, and the more I get to know you, the more I love you. I know one day you'll say it back."

He says it with such confidence that I can't help but ask, "How do you know?"

"You aren't the only one who talks to Papa," he says and grins.

CHAPTER THIRTY

After my walk with Uriah, he drops me off at home. We didn't get to walk long before the clouds came blowing in with a hard wind. I tell ya, living in Texas, the weather is mighty fickle. If I stop and think about it, maybe Papa made the weather so fickle so I'll stop wondering about the next moment and enjoy the one I'm in. I think on that as I change into my pajamas.

I feel like Papa needs my time and a word with me, so I grab a soda out of the fridge and sit in my chair with my feet up.

Uriah got me watermelon soda this time and, boy, is it good.

The clouds make the sky look angry. What with the lightning flashing and the thunder rolling. To me, it's pretty. Kinda like natural fireworks.

The woods are quiet. The animals normally out singing are hiding in their holes as the wind whips and whistles in the trees, waiting for this thing to pass. I've got my hair scrunchied so it stays out of my face, and this wind feels like it's bringing change.

Papa takes a seat next to me. He's watching His own handiwork with me.

"You gonna talk, or you just gonna sit there?" I ask Him.

The turbulence dies a moment, like it's checking its gas, making sure it's got enough to show me what for.

Papa looks at me and smiles. "I see you're talking to Uriah more. Letting him get to know you."

"Yeah, I like Uriah. He doesn't ask for anything from me."

"No, he doesn't. He loves you."

"I know." But hearing Papa say it makes it different.

"You love him."

"I don't." I snap.

Warmth spreads through my body and squeezes my heart. Papa and I haven't talked like this in a while. Not since that night with Bo. "Lilly, you can't lie to me. I know your heart. I know your wants. I know everything there is to know about you. Besides, you've already said you felt love for him once."

I look away. "I know you know me, but it was a moment of weakness. I don't love Uriah, though. You're wrong."

"You do. You love him like he's the best pie in the world."

I cut my eyes to Papa. "What do you know about pie?"

"I know it's your favorite thing, just like Uriah is your favorite thing."

"He is my favorite thing next to pie."

"Then why don't you let yourself love him?"

Because he deserves better love than what I have to offer. "Papa, you know as well as I do that I'm no good for him. All those people in town, flapping their gums, throwing judgment at him 'cause of me."

"Uriah doesn't seem to care about that."

"I do. You should too."

Papa pauses and sits real still. The storm that had quieted down a moment ago pulls back the throttle and lets loose. The wind howls, the sky flashes with lightning, and the thunder booms like bombs are being set off. Little bits of dead leaves and sticks are pelting me, and I shield my face.

"I made you mad?" I ask.

"I'm not mad at all. It's a storm. Hot air

meets cold air, pressure builds, and it has to let go."

"Why here?"

"You seem to be doing fine."

I nod and smile. "Your lessons sting sometimes."

"They sting because sometimes people are hard of hearing."

"Maybe they aren't hard of hearing, but they just don't like what you got to say. Ever think of that?"

The wind dies down, but the lightning and thunder still go on.

"Oh, I'm sure people don't like to hear a lot of what I say, as evidenced by the way people do things, thinking their way is better than mine."

"You trying to say I think that way?"

"You try to listen better than some, but you're still deaf at times."

I look down at the soda bottle I'm holding. More times than I can remember, I haven't been deaf; I've just been unwilling to listen. "I'm scared, Papa. The people I've tried to love, they ruined me on love. I'm afraid if I love Uriah that he'll do the same thing."

"You know that's not true."

"I don't. He already walked away once."

"Lilly, Uriah is a man, and he's not perfect. There will be times when he says the wrong thing or does the wrong thing, but he loves you. There will be times when you don't like him or feel anything for him because he's made you mad. You're just going to have to remember that I'm in the middle. You're going to have to remember to love him like I love him."

I take a deep breath. "Papa, why is this so hard? This love stuff?"

"If it were easy, then it wouldn't be worth having."

Papa and I sit for a long time on the deck, just watching the storm. When it starts to blow on us, we go inside, and He sits with me in my bedroom. Papa knows it takes me a while to come around, and He's patient. It makes me love Him more because He doesn't pressure me to just flip a switch.

While I'm lying in bed, I reflect on our talk. He says I love Uriah. It's hard to say those words. Of all the words I know, those three are the worst. They come out with so much hope. There's a promise in those words, and when those words aren't backed up, it's like being thrown into a fire. It burns you up and makes you hurt and wish you were dead.

I roll over onto my back and look up at the ceiling. "What do I do, Papa?"

Papa smiles. I feel His warmth fill the room, and it's like being in a fresh-out-of-the-dryer blanket. "You love. Not because you expect things to be good or perfect. You love because I love you. You love and remember that other people are just as broken as you are. You love and keep on loving, and you never stop."

"I can try."

"Do I ever ask you to do more than that?"

I hesitate. "Sometimes."

Papa laughs. It sings in my heart and makes me smile. "Sometimes I push you to more than try because I know you're capable of so much more. Sometimes I let you think you'll try just so you try and know what I've known all along."

"Okay, Papa. I think I understand."

"Good night, my sweet Lilly."

"Good night, Papa."

I roll over, tuck my hands under my pillow, and close my eyes. My talk with Papa has worn me out.

CHAPTER THIRTY-ONE

The next afternoon, after I've slept past what most people would call midmorning, I'm getting dressed because Uriah is coming over to take me for a walk around the pond. He's promised ice cream and good conversation.

I'm in the bathroom, looking in the mirror, and I realize for the first time in a while that I actually see myself. It takes me by surprise. It's been a long time since I've really taken a hard look. I've got a heart-shaped face, thin lips, and a seemingly proportionate nose. That said, I don't look half bad when I think about it. I'm not saying I'm pretty by any stretch, but I'd have to wear a mask at Halloween if I want to scare anybody.

When I finish my once-over, I walk out of the bathroom, and as I get to the living room, there's a knock on the door. Uriah's early, and it makes my heart smile. If only he knew what he means to me.

In my mind, Papa speaks, but I interrupt Him. "I know, Papa. Just give me time."

I'm not paying attention, and as I open the door, I say, "Hey, Uriah," but it's not Uriah. My face falls, and I'm standing directly in front of my daddy. I can smell cigarettes and alcohol pouring off him. His face is scraggly, and his clothes look like he's been sleeping in them for a few days.

What really scares me is the look on his face. A furrowed brow, red-rimmed eyes, and a twisted mouth tell me he's about to pay me back for all those times I've smarted back, caused him grief, and, most of all, for stabbing him in Thriftway.

I try to slam the door, but he uses the force of his entire body to push it open, so I turn to run. He kicks me in the butt, and I sprawl out on the floor. I try to scramble up, and he kicks me again, cracking my head on the coffee table. My ears ring, and the world spins.

Touching my head, I find there's a fair amount of blood. When I try to stand again, Daddy grabs a handful of my hair and slaps me across the face. "I told you, girl. I told you I'd get you one day, and today is my day." He grabs me by my chin, his fingernails digging into my skin, and puts his face in mine.

"You better go, Daddy. Uriah should be here any time, and if he..." With the way Daddy is holding my face, it comes out muddled.

Letting go of my hair, Daddy strikes me across the face with his fist, and I fall to the floor. I try to crawl away. I think if I can get somewhere, maybe I can fight back or hide or something, but Daddy's got different plans. He's come with a force I've been running from for years.

As I crawl, Daddy kicks me in the stomach. That's when I know for sure he's come to hurt me and hurt me good. He's got his pointed boots on, and that point connects with one of my ribs, snapping it.

I hear a rattle of tiny metal and the zip of a belt being pulled out of pant loops. I drag my eyes up to his face, and what I see is hatred. He hates me. He's hated me for a long time. I just don't know why.

"Daddy, why do you hate me?"

He stops and looks at me, confused for a second like he's never even given it a moment's thought. Then he pulls his arm back. I hold up my hand, trying to keep the belt from hitting, but it lands around my arm and across my back with a smack. "Your mouth. That's why. You always had to talk like you knew better than me."

He reaches back, and the belt comes down hard again. "You always talked like you were better than me. You were nothing but dirt, just like your drug-addict daddy. I hated him too. Your face just reminds me of his face. I tried to love you, but every time I looked at your face, it was just your ornery, dirty daddy looking back at me."

"Daddy, I'm sorry. I'm sorry. Please stop!"

"Too late, girl."

After that, I guess he's explained all he's going to explain, because he hits me with the belt again and again and again, punctuated with kicks each time. Daddy kicks me so hard that I come up off the floor and land with a thud each time.

It's funny…I'm lying there, and I realize

two things. One, my daddy is going to beat me to death, and, two, of all the times to remember something, I remember why I stabbed him in Thriftway. Now I can tell Chrissy what happened. A giggle slips out at the thought.

Daddy grabs me by the hair again to pull me up off the floor. I've got no strength to help, so my head feels like it's being scalped. He digs his fingers into my chin again.

I can't really see his face. My vision is blurry either from the beating or the blood. He slaps me again, but I don't feel much at this point.

I'm dazed. Daddy starts talking, and it sounds like he's in a wind tunnel. "Your momma always tried to come between me and you. Always tried to explain your smart mouth," he says as his spittle hits my lips and cheeks.

He levels his gaze at me and smiles a sinister smile, making me wish I'd never been born. "I knew what Marlin was doing to you. You and your momma thought I didn't, but I did. Your momma whooped you 'cause she thought she was keeping me outta jail, but she didn't know I knew. I knew, and I was glad it was happening. Your high-and-mighty rear-end getting what was coming to ya 'cause your momma wouldn't let me whip you like I wanted." He shoves me back against the wall with his hand squeezing my throat.

I try to claw at his hands, gasping for air. My lungs are burning as he watches me fight, getting joy from it.

When he lets go, I land hard on the floor. I'm coughing, trying to get air as my ears ring and my head swims. I can't do anything but lie there while Daddy begins beating me again. Every ounce of my strength is gone.

I vaguely make out that Uriah's come in the door.

Daddy's cussin' and shoutin'.

There's a scuffle.

Then Uriah is cradling me, brushing the hair off my face and speaking softly. "Oh, my Lilly. Oh, my sweet Lilly."

I blink a few times, but my vision is still fuzzy.

"The ambulance is on the way, Lilly. You hold on. You hear me?"

I'm numb and can taste blood in my mouth. It makes me wonder what's bleedin' on the inside. It's hard to concentrate, and a thought comes to my mind: I'm dying.

I've spent all this time with Uriah, scared to death to feel anything. I've kept him at arm's length because other people have hurt me and I'm afraid of him doing the same. He's been nothing but good to me, and I've treated him like people have treated me.

There's excited movement in the living room, and I hear muffled voices.

The need to tell Uriah before I go is overwhelming. "Uriah, I love you. I love you with all my heart."

I don't know if I've said it loud enough for Uriah to hear me or what. Whatever Daddy's done to me, he's done it good and proper, and I can't stay anymore.

CHAPTER THIRTY-TWO

As I wake up, I put together that I'm in a hospital. Everything is quiet and serene, minus a few chirping noises here and there. It smells sterile and clean.

I ache all over.

My left arm is in a cast, every breath I take burns, and when I look down with the one eye that isn't so swollen, any visible skin is covered in bruises in varying shades of black and purple. My throat is sore, and my mouth is dry, so when I try to speak, it comes out as a grunt.

Uriah is haloed by the light as he moves to stand over me.

I peer up with my one good eye. "Hi," I whisper. "I guess I'm not dead."

"Hi," he says, and his voice cracks. "Not for a lack of trying. That's for sure."

"Are you okay?"

"Am I okay?" he asks and sits on the edge of the bed. "No, I'm not."

"Did Daddy get you too?"

"He hurt you, and that was all it took."

"I hurt, Uriah."

I know he's pressed the nurse call button when I hear a voice speak and say, "Can I help you?"

"She's hurting," Uriah says.

"We'll be there in a moment."

"Where is my daddy?"

"He's sitting in jail at the moment."

"Jail?"

"Yep. The police picked him up after he left the cabin. Bo got pictures of you when they first brought you in and showed them to Judge Kringle. He's going to be there for a while."

"Bo was here?"

"Yeah, he saw you and broke down crying. He took pictures and left without saying much of anything."

"They won't keep my daddy. Judge Kringle has known him a long time. He could've killed me, and he'd still not have to worry about jail."

"Well, they have him in there, so Judge Kringle must think something."

"It's a formality. He'll be out in no time."

"He's been there three days so far."

"Three days? I've been out three days?"

"Your dad worked you over pretty good. You've got three broken ribs on the right side and one broken rib and three cracked ribs on the left. It's a pure miracle you didn't bleed internally."

"I thought it was you. I thought you'd

come by early. I opened the door without looking. He came in so fast and furious that I didn't have time to get away. I just wasn't expecting him at the cabin, at all." I shift and immediately wish I hadn't. The pain makes me breathless.

Uriah pushes the button again and reminds the nurse that I'm still hurting.

"I probably should go so you can rest."

I grab his hand, the idea of him leaving throwing me into a panic. "Please don't go, Uriah. Please, don't. Don't leave me here. I know Daddy is in jail, but people know him. They like him, and I just know he won't stay there." Tears pool in my eyes. I don't know if it's the thought of being alone or the idea that I wasn't going to see him again.

"I don't need an explanation as to why you want me to stay. I'll stay. Momma should be up after a while. She's been coming by and staying when I go home, take a shower, and eat." Uriah leans down and kisses me on the forehead.

"I think Daddy came to kill me," I confess. "If you hadn't been picking me up, he'd have done it, too."

Uriah straightens. "I wish I could disagree, but with what I saw, I know you're right. He wouldn't take me on, though. He thought he could, but I tossed his rear out the door and called the police. He high-tailed it as soon as I dialed the number."

"It won't matter. You just wait. He'll find a way out."

Uriah shakes his head. "I don't think so. I think he's in trouble this time."

"You don't know my daddy or his friends. You don't know how mean he is."

"You give him too much power." Uriah wants to take my hand, but he also doesn't want to hurt me, so he braces his hand on the bed and leans over me.

I can't seem to make him understand.

My daddy has power in this small town. They all knew what he was like, but it was an unspoken truth. It was the "smile to your face and stab you in the back" type of knowing. "You don't give him enough."

"Lilly, he's in trouble," he insists.

"Momentarily, sure, but you don't know. You don't know him like I do."

Uriah looks at me, eyebrows furrowed and lips pressed together tight. "You're really scared of him getting out."

"I think I have reason to be. That day in Thriftway, I was helping him do some grocery shopping. We were going to go home, and he was going to cook dinner for me. I don't know what either of us said, but he said something, and I was trying to be funny. He took it like I was bein' a smart mouth. He grabbed me by the hair and told me he was sick of my smart mouth."

Uriah's eyes widen, and his lips part.

The memory is back, and it's playing in

color. "We were looking at cups because he'd broken his favorite one. He had one in his hand, and he reached back with it and looked around to make sure no one was looking. He was going to hit me with it. It's why I stabbed him. I fought against him 'cause he was going to hurt me. I knew right then he was going to hurt me and hurt me bad. He didn't care where we were."

"And you forgot that?"

"I think I was trying to protect myself. I didn't want to think my own daddy wanted to hurt me. It bothers me to think that the people who were supposed to love me didn't. Momma tried to love me, but she loved Daddy more, and she would protect him over me. It was war in my house most of the time. Momma keeping Daddy from me, and me trying to survive. It's why I ran from here. It's why it's hard to be here. All those memories. All those things that happened."

What builds in my chest pains me like nothing I've felt, and I begin to sob. "Mr. Marlin still looks at me like I'm a piece of trash. Daddy told me he knew about Mr. Marlin." I can't decide if I'm brokenhearted because my daddy hates me or because my daddy knew someone was hurting me and didn't care.

Uriah gently puts his arms around me and holds me against him. "You break my heart, Lillian James. No one ever deserves to be treated like that, least of all you."

CHAPTER THIRTY-THREE

Between Uriah and his momma, I have someone with me at all times while I'm in the hospital. The first few days after I come to, I'm so sore I can barely breathe. My daddy has worked me over, and every square inch of me feels it.

I'm lying in bed on the fifth day, and Uriah is slouched down in the chair with his feet on the sofa when Dr. Sands comes in. He greets me with a smile and glances down at the chart he's holding.

Uriah stands and shakes his hand.

"How are you feeling?" Dr. Sands asks and checks the monitors attached to me.

"'Bout as good as a fresh bruise is supposed to feel, I guess."

"Well, you're going to feel sore for a while. Do you have someone to stay with while you recover?"

I start to say something, and Uriah speaks up. "Yes, sir, she does." He looks at me.

"Well, I think we can discharge you today. I've got some prescriptions I'm gonna send you home with, mostly for pain. You'll need to check in with your primary doctor to get your cast removed in six weeks."

"Yes, sir," I say.

"A nurse will be in after a while with some papers to sign, and you'll be free to go," he says and smiles before walking out the door.

I look at Uriah. "You know I can't stay with you. People will talk, and I won't have them saying hateful things about you and your momma."

Uriah puts his hands on his hips with a look of defiance. "I don't care what anyone says. You've stayed your last time at the cabin. We have a big enough house that you can have your own room, and Momma will make sure nothing funny is going on."

"I just don't feel right about it." I'm still not used to the cast, and I bump my head with it and wince. "Stupid cast. I can't wait to get this thing off."

"Lilly, no one is going to say anything. You need time to heal, and someone has to take care of you. Believe me, if Momma had a problem with you, you'd know it."

I shake my head and look down. "I hate that all this has happened. It's like I can't get away from trouble. I hurt everyone around me."

"You haven't hurt anyone. If anything, you're the one who's been hurt."

I look at him, frustrated beyond belief. "Yeah, but all my problems…all this stuff is bleeding outside the edges and touching the people I love."

Uriah smiles. "People?"

I bite my lip. It's not like I've forgotten what I said that day. I remember it, but I haven't said it again. I think it was easier to say when I thought there wasn't a chance for disappointment. Now, I'm alive and kicking, and the words rest on the end of my tongue and refuse to budge.

"Yes, people."

"I heard you that day," Uriah says. "Don't think I didn't."

I can't meet his eyes. I'm ashamed and embarrassed that I can't say it again.

He sits on the edge of the bed, tips my chin until I'm looking him in the eyes, and smiles. "I'm going to go home and get things ready for you. Will you be okay alone a little while?"

"I will."

He bends down and kisses my forehead. I've come to enjoy those little kisses. It's like he's telling me everything is going to be okay with just a simple touch.

He stands and walks to the door.

"Would you mind shutting the door?" I ask. "Papa and I need to talk."

He smiles and slips out the door, shutting it behind him.

I lie back on the bed and close my eyes. I still hurt pretty much everywhere. I think I've even got a bruise on my pinky toe.

"Papa?" I can't feel Him, and I haven't talked to Him since Daddy put me in the hospital. "Papa, please come talk to me." I reach for Him, and it's like He's just out of arm's reach.

I cover my face with my hands, making sure not to conk myself with my stupid cast. The tears pouring down my face feel like a waterfall. "Papa, please come talk to me. I need you to talk to me. Please."

It feels like He's not coming. I'm alone, and I feel emptier than I have in years. At this point, I'm hopeless. Papa's not coming. Somehow, I've pushed Him away, and I'm in this desert with no signs of life.

It hurts to cry like this too. That deep-down-ache type of cry that wears you out and makes you feel like you've been climbing a mountain. It would hurt without all the bruises, but with them, the pain is unbelievable.

Just when I think Papa has decided not to show up, I feel Him park Himself in the chair right by my bed. "Hello, Lilly," He says.

"Where have you been, Papa? I've been calling and calling. Didn't you hear me?" I ask through sobs. It feels like my soul is physically bleeding.

"I heard you. I'm here. I just needed your heart open."

"I hurt Papa." It comes out more like a wail.

"I know, sweetest. I know." His voice is soft and comforting.

"Did you know Daddy hated me?"

"I did."

I'm gobsmacked. Papa knew? "Then why did you give me to him?"

Papa shakes His head. "I didn't."

"You didn't stop it."

"I couldn't. I can't take away free will. If I'd stopped it, what do you think would have happened? Do you think Lucy and Will would have changed?"

"No, but there had to be better people who could raise me."

Papa sits quietly a second. "Lilly, they had choices to make, and they didn't ask me. They didn't want me. People have to want me and my best for them. Forcing people to do anything isn't a relationship. I want a relationship, Lilly. I want to be the desire of your heart. I can't force that. I won't."

My shoulders sag. "But you could have guided them to a different choice."

"I can guide them, but I can't force them to use my guidance."

I sigh in frustration. "But you've made me a compost heap. I'm a mess."

"A beautiful, wonderful heap. The most beautiful things grow out of a compost heap. Just think of all the flower seeds you're sowing. Chrissy talks to me more. I've loved her for so long, and now we spend early mornings together before she opens her practice. Bo's been talking to me this week too. I've got work to do with him, but his heart is open and wide. Uriah always talked to me, but now the way he talks to me is so much better."

"I need a break, Papa. I need some peace. I need some time to not hurt."

Papa takes a deep breath. "I know, but this world is hard. I can't guarantee you won't hurt or get hurt."

"Can I just have a little time, though? Just a little time? I'm so tired of all of this."

"I know, sweetest. Give me your faith, Lilly. The faith that I have nothing but good planned, even in the darkness. I can tell you I love you, and I am with you. I'll be here to comfort and care for your heart."

We sit quietly for a moment. I can't stop being weepy. "I can't seem to tell Uriah I love him now that I know I'm not dying."

"I know. I was here."

Casting a quick glance at Him, I say, "I didn't feel you here."

"I'm more than a feeling, and you know that. I'm always here."

"Sometimes I feel like you leave me. I feel like you leave me when I need you the most. Like when Daddy was beating on me."

"I was there. I saw it." Papa's arms wrap around me as the room grows warmer. "It broke my heart. I hated to see you being hurt like that."

"Why does he hate me?" I whisper, not sure I'm ready for the answer. A child wanting a parent's love and knowing it'll never happen is a hard reality to face.

"My love, he hates you, he hates me, he hates everyone, and he takes it out on you."

"Why does he hate you?" It doesn't make sense to me. My daddy was around church people all his life. My mama, near the end, for sure would have done all she could to make sure he made it to heaven.

"Oh, for a myriad of reasons."

"I don't know a lot about my daddy other than he was mean. From the way Momma talked about him, he had a pretty hard life growing up. You'd think he wouldn't wish that on someone else."

"You'd think so, but sometimes people are so broken that they don't realize I'm what they're looking for. They think hurting others will make their pain go away when it just makes it worse."

I hear a light tap on the door, and it's a nurse. She comes in, takes out my IV, and then has me sign a few papers.

"When your boyfriend gets back, you'll be free to go, okay?" She smiles sweetly at me. I should tell her he's not my boyfriend, but it seems like arguing for argument's sake.

I wait for her to leave, and then I say, "I'm tired, Papa. I'm tired all the way down deep."

"I know."

"I love Uriah." My talk with Papa feels like a windy mountain road. The kind where you feel like you're meeting the road you just came from.

"I know that too."

"I'm gonna rest a bit, Papa. I love you too."

"I know, Lilly. I'll see you later."

I'm plumb exhausted at this point. I close my eyes to rest, and sleep comes quicker than it ever has before.

CHAPTER THIRTY-FOUR

The first few days at Uriah's are hard on me. For one thing, I don't like being there. Not that I'm not grateful, but I'm right about people talking. For another, it feels weird. I didn't like it last time, and this time I'm staying even longer.

Uriah's house is different than anyone's on the block. It's older too. From what I've gathered from talking to Mrs. Pendleton, her big old farmhouse was passed down to her through the generations.

Foaming Springs was a good ten or

twenty miles away, and over time, it just kinda spread in the direction of the house. Now there are a few houses around them. It still isn't like a regular neighborhood. Like the house I grew up in, with sidewalks and neighbors you could almost touch.

This house is enough distance from other houses that it's comfortable. I love their porch. It's big, like the movies. I've started going out in the evening, sitting in one of the big rocking chairs and watching the horses across the way. It's fun to watch them run and play with each other.

They won't let me do anything yet, so I'm sitting out on the porch, enjoying the sun and the breeze, when Mrs. Pendleton sits in the rocking chair next to me. "See anything interesting?"

I look at her and smile. "All of it's interesting to me. I like to sit outside."

"Me too. Uriah's finishing up the dishes.

I asked him to fix the front fence tonight. It's bugging the daylights out of me."

The fence she's talking about is a white picket fence that runs in front of the house and down the sides. It's just tall enough to need a gate and just short enough that it doesn't block the view.

"He likes to work with his hands," I reply.

Mrs. Pendleton is looking out over the horizon like me. "Yeah, he does. Gets that from his daddy. I suspect here soon he'll start his own business. He's been working on houses in town here and there. Doing real good work. Getting calls for more work."

I glance at her. "Does he regret getting out of the Army too early?"

She shakes her head. "Nah, he was done. He was coming home to find you."

"He told you that?" My mouth drops open, and I look at her in shock.

"My boy and I talk a lot, sugar." She winks.

Sugar, that's what Mrs. Pendleton calls me. I don't know why 'cause most people say I'm anything but sweet.

I get my wits back pretty quick. "He deserves better than me. I've told him so."

Mrs. Pendleton stops rocking and places her hand on mine. "Look at me, sugar."

I do what I'm told.

"Who says you're not good enough?" she asks with a chuckle.

Looking her in the eyes is hard. "No one has to say it. I just know."

She pats my hand. "Well, you don't know anything."

I feel tiny. "I just know my family isn't good."

"Listen," she says and starts rocking again. "Family is family. We can't change where we come from, but we aren't defined by it. Sugar, I've watched you grow up. I knew your mama, and I know your daddy. You've turned out pretty good if you ask me."

"I'm not sure they'd agree."

"Well, they'd be wrong, then. A real daddy don't beat his baby like he beat you. You're not the trash, sugar. You're the flower that grew up in the midst of trash."

I turn so she can't see the tears in my eyes. Her words are nearly the same as Papa's. "No one's ever talked to me like that. Except maybe Uriah."

"My boy's been sweet on you for a long, long time. He's talked about you for as long as I can remember."

"I had a crush on him in school. All the way through." Not like I can hide that. "I remember the first day I saw him in first grade."

"But you don't remember much about being little in this town, do you?"

I shake my head. "No, most of the bad is what fills my mind."

Mrs. Pendleton grunts a laugh. "Well, let me tell you some good. Maybe we can erase that bad." I like how she's always sunshine and sees the good in things.

"You remember things about me?"

"Oh, sugar, I sure do. You were the only little who would come in the kitchen and want to help with the potlucks. You'd ask to help, and your momma would snap at you. You'd go to the corner and just bawl. I'd find you and get you working on something. You'd never complain about the job, either."

"I don't remember that, Mrs. Pendleton."

"You were also the first one to say hello to someone new."

"I was?"

"Uriah told me that. He'd come home with a Lilly story all the time. How you'd helped someone or sat with someone who wasn't as popular. Sugar, you were a sweet little thing."

"I truly have no memory of that." There are a lot of holes in my memory it seems.

"Well, I guess it's a good thing you get to stay here a while, then, huh?" As Mrs. Pendleton finishes saying that, Uriah comes stomping out the front door and stops. There's a big tool belt strapped around his waist.

He smiles at the two of us. "I'm gonna work on the fence now. Okay, Momma?"

"Okay, honey. Make sure to get the gate too. I'm sick of that thing squeaking."

Uriah smiles and winks at me, and then he trots off to the fence to work on it.

Mrs. Pendleton looks over at me and smiles. "Uriah doesn't want you at that cabin anymore. Says it's not safe."

"I know, but it doesn't feel right being here. I don't want the town to say hateful things about you and him."

"Sugar, you worry too much about what other people say. Let 'em talk. What goes on in this house is between me, you, Uriah, and Papa." She gives me a pointed look.

My mouth drops open. "He's told you about that?"

"First time you told him. He came home telling me all about it."

"You think I'm squirrelly too?"

She crosses her arms over her chest and stares ahead to where Uriah's working. "Nah, I think you're one of the few people in this town who does more than go to church."

"I don't go to church."

"You can start coming with me and Uriah. Anyone says anything, and I'll hit 'em with my purse." She winks at me.

"You know about that too?"

"Of course. It was the talk of the town for weeks. Your wild momma crackin' someone over the head for that mean-as-a-snake man."

I twist in my seat and look at her. "You know Daddy is mean?"

She scoffs. "Sugar, I grew up here. Lived here all my life. I was here before your momma came to live here. I know a lot of things about a lot of stuff."

"You know my daddy knows a lot of people, then. When he gets out, he's going to come for me." I stop rocking. The idea that my daddy can get out and come after me scares me. There's just no better word for it.

"He knows a lot of people, but all those people he knows have been fooled by his slick tongue. I saw you right after you got to the hospital. If people see what I saw, he'll be lucky he doesn't get the electric chair."

"I doubt it. He's good at getting out of

things." I look forward and begin rocking again.

Mrs. Pendleton shakes her head. "No, sugar, not this time. This time, he's got a reckonin' coming. This time, he's got to answer for his actions."

"I wish I could be certain like you."

"He's brainwashed you and terrorized you since you were little. Always did make me fightin' mad that a man like him could have a sweet thing like you."

"I'm not all that sweet, Mrs. Pendleton."

"You hush. I know you are. I don't know if you remember this or not, but one time I caught your daddy beating the tar out of you behind the church. You were screaming your little heart out. I swooped down and grabbed you. To this day, I still don't know why he was whooping you like that."

I've realized that there are things that happened to me when I was little that I can't remember. I don't remember him doing that, but I believe Mrs. Pendleton. She wouldn't say it if it wasn't so. "I asked Daddy when he was beating on me why he hated me."

"What'd he say?"

"He said it's 'cause I look like Will. He hated Will because he was trash and I was trash too." I chew on the inside of my cheek and wipe my eyes.

Mrs. Pendleton purses her lips and shakes her head. "Worthless man. He doesn't know how blessed he is. I lost two babies before Uriah. The last one was a girl, stillborn. I wanted a girl so bad. I wanted to braid her hair, dress her in pretty dresses, and love on her. It's what made me so mad that your momma and daddy got you. I never could understand how God could give a sweet'ems like you to them and take mine from me, but then I had Uriah." She wipes her eyes with the sleeve of her dress. "That boy is the best thing I ever had. He's sweet and kind. And now he's brought me home the little I've loved since the first time I saw her."

I put my hand over my mouth. I can't believe what I'm hearing. "You can't be talking about me."

"Sugar, you were mine from the moment I saw you. I've prayed over you every day since you were little. When you left here, I prayed for God to watch over you, to love you, and to work in a way to bring you back. Uriah don't know none of this, but I wanted you to know. I don't want you thinking you have to leave anytime soon or that I don't think you're good enough."

Oh, Papa, what have you done?

Through the tears, I say, "You mean you wanted me?"

"Oh, sugar, yes. Funny thing is, Ray and I was done after one. That's all we wanted. So, if my little girl had made it, I wouldn't have Uriah. Now I've got Uriah *and* you."

I can't believe my ears. "I don't know what to say."

"Nothing to say. I thought we needed to have a talk. I thought you needed to know. Now you do. I love you to pieces, Lillian Louise James." She reaches over and pats me on the hand. Her face is streaked with tears, and she has a big smile. "It took a while, but I got everything I prayed for. Maybe not in my timing, and maybe not the way I wanted. But I got it."

"What's all this?" Uriah asks. I didn't even remember he was working on the fence. He's drenched in sweat, his hair sticking against his head and his shirt soaked.

"Oh, nothing, just me and Lilly talking. You thirsty?" Mrs. Pendleton asks and stands.

Uriah looks between us, and I can see the wheels turning. He's wondering what's been said. No doubt, he'll ask as soon as he can. "I could use something."

She smiles and walks into the house without saying anything.

Uriah sits in the same chair she was using and looks at me, curious. "What's with the tears? Why's my momma crying?"

I shake my head. "That's between us."

"Come on." He taps me with his fingers.

"No."

His mouth drops open, but his lips turn up at the corners. "You're really not gonna tell me, are ya?"

I shake my head again.

He sits back in the chair and wipes his forehead with his hand. "It's not fair, you keeping secrets with my momma."

About that time, the screen door knocks open, and Mrs. Pendleton comes out with three glasses of water. "Something you ain't meant to know, son."

Uriah pops out of the chair and gives it

back to his momma, and she hands him a glass and then me. I take a long drink, and Uriah is still looking at us both like he can't believe we'd keep a secret from him. "That's not fair."

"Little about life is fair," she says as she sits.

Uriah drains his glass, wipes his mouth, and goes back to the fence, looking back and grumbling.

"Mrs. Pendleton?"

"Yes?"

"Why did you want me? I don't remember coming to your house or being around you much."

"Your momma didn't like me. We had words about you more than a few times. I told her I didn't like the way your daddy did things, and she didn't like my opinions."

"You?" I can't grasp someone not outright loving Mrs. Pendleton.

"Sugar, I'm not one to hold my opinions

when I see a baby being mistreated. You stayed here a few times."

I stare at the ground, trying to think of spending time with the Pendletons. I can't. "I don't remember any of that."

"It don't surprise me. You had it rough. When you got older, people in this town didn't make it easy on you. You were friends with Bo, but I think he only stuck to you 'cause he was sweet on you. I didn't like the look of him at all."

"Uriah told you?"

"Uriah and I don't keep many secrets. Now that his daddy's gone, he confides in me even more."

"When did Mr. Pendleton pass?"

"A few years ago. We were going to bed one night, and he felt a sharp pain run down his arm. Next thing I knew, he was having a massive heart attack. There was nothing to be done. Uriah had just signed another contract for the Army. That's part of why he came home early. He knew I was here by myself."

"I'm sorry."

"Nah, sugar, don't be. Me and Ray, we had a long love affair. He was a good man. Only thing that burns me is how that daddy of yours gets to live a long life and my sweet Ray didn't. Why God lets some folks live long and others not so long baffles me at times."

"I don't understand Papa sometimes either."

"I think we all feel like that."

Colors begin to splash across the horizon as the sun gets lower in the sky. I feel more peace on this porch than I've felt...well, than I've ever felt. "I think some people feel it more than others."

Mrs. Pendleton laughs. "I bet those others feel the same way."

I chuckle, and the chuckle turns into a full-on laughing fit which feels great and hurts like crazy all at the same time.

Mrs. Pendleton glances at me, and she starts laughing too.

Uriah steps back up on the porch, still somewhat sore that we didn't tell him what we were talking about earlier. "More secrets."

"No, honey, we just don't understand Papa sometimes."

He sets his hands on his hips. "Me either. And I think some people feel it more than others."

Mrs. Pendleton and I cackle.

Uriah is standing there, looking at us like we've lost our marbles, but for once, the weight of the world doesn't seem to be weighing on my shoulders as heavy.

CHAPTER THIRTY-FIVE

The next Sunday, the three of us load up into Uriah's pickup for church. Mrs. Pendleton asked me to go, and there was no way I was telling her no. Uriah drives, she sits in the middle, and I get in last. My ribs still hurt a lot when I move, so crawling into a pickup is just not happening.

I haven't been to church since that Wednesday. I'd forgotten about being all bruised and swollen. People are already staring, and I haven't even gotten out of the pickup yet.

Uriah gets out and jogs around the front of the pickup to open the door and help me out and then his momma.

Together, we walk into the church. Pastor Jeffrey is standing at the door, shaking hands with people as they come in. He shakes Mrs. Pendleton's hand and tells her he's glad to see her, same with Uriah. When he gets to me, he pauses and then shakes my hand, not saying a word.

Of course, I like to sit in the farthest spot from the pulpit as possible, but that's not to be. I follow Uriah and his momma until we're about six rows from the pulpit. In the middle. Where the whole world can look on me and judge.

I'm so uncomfortable I could crawl under a rock, but I make sure my feelings are kept to myself. Mrs. Pendleton cares for me, and if she wants to sit here, then this is where I'll sit.

We aren't the first people here, but

when you go to church every Sunday and Wednesday for as long as Mrs. Pendleton has, people know which seats belong to you, and they make sure they're waiting for you when you get there.

The church is filling up as it gets closer to the time for Pastor Jeffrey to start preaching. Most are casting glances at me. It's the same, though. I grew up in this church, and I know all of them don't think much of me. Even if it wasn't my fault or choice.

I feel a tap on my shoulder, and Chrissy is sitting behind me. My ability to look at her is limited, so she leans forward, whispering in my ear, "You coming to see me tomorrow?"

"I guess."

"Good. I've missed our talks."

"As much as it pains me to say this, I do too."

Chrissy giggles and sits back. I can hear

her continue to giggle until Pastor Jeffery gets to the pulpit and asks Jenny to lead the singing.

I go to stand, but Uriah puts a hand on my shoulder and shakes his head. When I give him a look, the kind that says I need to follow the rules, he sits back down. "You don't need to stand," he whispers.

"I feel weird sitting."

"No one cares."

"Only because they like you."

He smiles. "They like you too. They just don't know it yet."

"Uriah, I know you want that, but it might never happen."

"You wait."

Afterward, we hush because people are watching us.

Once the singing part is over, Pastor Jeffrey gets up to the pulpit again. He preaches on forgiveness. I don't know if he's talking directly to me, but I know Papa is. I'm struggling with that. I haven't told anyone, but when your daddy comes to the house determined to snuff you, it can rip all the forgiveness right out of you.

Pastor Jeffrey talks about how if we don't forgive, then Papa can't forgive us. All in all, it's not much I haven't heard before, but I feel like Papa wants me to hear it again.

Papa, I hear you, and I will. I just need a little time.

My heart feels a little tug, and Papa says, *Don't hold on to your anger. It'll turn to bitterness and eat you from the inside out.*

I tell Papa, *I know. I'm working on it. I promise.*

When Pastor Jeffrey is done, he prays and dismisses us.

Mrs. Pendleton asks Uriah to help one of the older ladies out to her car. She got in okay, but now that she's sat still for so long on these hard pews, she's having trouble getting around. Both of them help her while I stay inside.

As soon as they're out of sight, Bo comes up to me. It feels a little awkward being around him. I'm not sure how much time will have to pass before that feeling will go away.

"Hi, Bo."

"Hey. You're looking way better."

"Well, how I see it, the only way I had to go was up."

Bo chuckles. "Already making jokes."

"I think if I stop, I'll cry." It sounds like a joke, but it's not far from the truth.

"You're about to be free from this little town. You ready?"

I shuffle my feet and look at the ground. "Oh, I doubt I'll ever be free from here."

"Well, you'll at least be allowed out of the town. Maybe you won't be stuck eating tacos or fish."

I hold my ribs as I laugh. "The tacos

aren't so bad as long as they're fresh. It's the next day when they bite ya."

"Your ribs still hurting, huh?" His gaze flicks to my body and back up.

Before I answer, I take a small breath. "Yeah, the doctor said they take a while to heal. He wasn't kidding."

He points to my hand. "When do you get your cast off?"

I lift it and rub it with my free hand. "Oh, the normal six weeks. I may have a concussion by the time I'm done wearing the thing, though. I keep conking myself in the head."

Bo's shoulders bounce up and down as he laughs. When he stops laughing, I feel the mood shift. Things are about to get serious.

"Lilly, I'm sorry. I should have never done what I did. It was wrong as wrong could be. I know I can't take it back or change it, but I hope one day we can be friends again. Just friends."

As we're talking, Becky Martin walks up and smiles at me before addressing Bo. "Hey, your momma said to come get you. We've got the choir loaded up and ready to go."

Bo looks at me. "The church is taking the choir to lunch over in the next town. Kind of a special treat. Daddy and Mr. Paul had a wager about the last Rangers game, and Daddy lost."

"Okay, well, you all have fun. I'll stay here."

When Bo and Becky walk off, I watch them. Sure enough, they hold hands just before they get out the door. I knew he didn't love me. It was just a matter of him knowing it too.

It's the second week of August in Texas, which means it's H O T, hot. Uriah comes walking up to me, and he looks like he's about to melt. "What are you smiling about?" he asks, out of breath.

I shrug. "Oh, nothing."

"You gonna start keeping secrets from me?" He chuckles.

"I don't think it's a secret."

His eyebrows knit together. "Then what?"

I tip my head in the direction Bo and Becky went. "Bo's going with Becky Martin."

He makes a humming sound and nods. "Oh, that? Yeah, I knew. It started about two weeks ago. She always liked him."

"I know."

Uriah smiles. "You and him friends again?"

"No, but I think after a while we might be." And it's not feeling as hard as it did a few weeks ago. "You look hot."

A bead of sweat trickles down the side

of Uriah's face. "I am hot. You ready to go? Momma's waiting in the truck."

Chrissy's husband, Phillip, is closing the church up today, and I see him with his hand on the small of her back. She sees me and smiles as Uriah and I are walking out of the church.

Misty Morning is standing there with her, and for once, she doesn't give me the stink eye. I doubt we'll ever be friends, but maybe, just maybe, she won't hate me as much anymore. I guess church is full of surprises after all.

CHAPTER THIRTY-SIX

I wake up in the middle of the night, drenched in sweat, and panting like I've been running for my life. My mouth is dry, so I go to the kitchen and get something to drink. I'm wide awake, and instead of heading back to the bedroom, I go outside and sit on the porch.

It's not as dark on Uriah's porch as it is on mine, and there's not near as much animal life. Of course, there are frogs and crickets everywhere you go, so they're making noise. The moon is shining bright, casting shadows here and there.

The rocking chair is so much louder at night than it is in the daylight. I'm sitting, drinking my glass of water and watching the world, when I feel Papa sit down next to me. I'm not sure I'm ready to talk to Him. That's when I realize I'm mad at Him.

"I don't want to talk to you right now." I set my glass on the porch.

"I know."

"Then why are you here?" I snap.

"Because I want to talk to you."

"What if I don't want to listen?"

"I know you. You do."

"No, I don't," I say in a huff. "I don't want to talk to you, and I don't want to hear what you have to say."

"That's not true." His voice is soft and wraps around my heart enough that I'm choked by the emotion that hits me.

I slide down in the rocker and sulk. "Why you gotta be so…you?"

"Lilly, I know you're hurt."

"Yeah, and you let me get hurt."

At first, after Daddy beat me, I didn't think I was mad, but my emotions and feelings have been all over the place in the time since. I feel like Papa allowed all this bad stuff to happen to me, and if He loved me, He would've protected me. If He loved me, He wouldn't keep letting all this bad stuff happen to me.

"I didn't let you get hurt. This world is broken, and there are broken people in it."

"Yeah, but you could've protected me. Done something." Not that I could hide my anger before, but I'm not even trying to be polite now.

"Lilly, just because I didn't stop it doesn't mean I don't love you. If I stopped everything bad from happening to everyone then I would have to stop everyone from doing anything bad. That would be taking away everyone's free will. Sometimes I fix things and sometimes I don't. It's impossible for you to understand why without being me."

"I don't want to talk to you, Papa. I want to be angry. I deserve to be angry. I deserve to hate and let it make me bitter, and I deserve justice. I deserve revenge." I cover my eyes with my hand and stop rocking. I hurt so profoundly that I can't find words to describe the level of anguish I feel. My whole body is shaking with the anger that's consuming me.

"Well, you can be angry, but what will it help?"

My words are lodged in my throat, and I grip the arms of the rocking chair tighter.

Papa's Spirit is swirling around me, and I can feel the warmth of it. "Lilly, those people sinned against me. I'm the one who delivers the vengeance and the justice, because when I deliver it, it will be pure and just."

"Papa, please," I cry. "I don't want to do this right now."

"Why?"

"Because." I say through gritted teeth.

"Because why?"

"I don't know."

"Why do you want to keep all this hurt? What will it help?"

That rooted anger gets a little more fertilizer and shoots roots through me. "Because I think I should get to wave my anger like a banner so the world can see all the bad things that have happened in my life. So they can see I've survived and I'm happy despite all that bad stuff that's happened to me."

"But are you happy?"

"No."

"Then what's the point of hanging on to

all that anger and bitterness if it's really not getting you what you want?"

I bang my casted hand on the rocker arm. "It's not fair, Papa. It's not fair that I'm afraid and hurt. It's not fair that Daddy gets to hurt me, and I have to suffer. I want him to suffer like I am. I want him to hurt like I am. I want him to pay for all the years of hating me and hurting me, and I want...revenge."

"Lilly?" Mrs. Pendleton calls from the door.

I wipe my eyes and try to control my voice. "Yes, ma'am."

The door creaks open, and then the thin, flimsy screen door shuts. She stands behind me. "You okay, sugar?"

I start to open my mouth to say something, but the words are drowned out with a sob.

"Oh, sugar, come here." She pulls me out of the rocker and hugs me tight, trying to soothe me. "Oh, sugar, I know you must hurt something fierce. I know you must wonder why no one has ever protected you, but I'm here. I'm here now."

My sobs turn into an aching weep as my knees give out, and I pull her down onto the floor of the porch with me. Mrs. Pendleton sits, rocking me, smoothing my hair and speaking softly. I don't know how long we sit like that, but by the time I'm finished crying, my bones are sore. Sitting on the hardwood floor of the porch is not smart when you're still bruised.

"I heard what you said, Lilly."

"You think less of me?"

"Oh, no, sugar," she says softly, continuing to smooth my hair. "Everyone feels like that from time to time. You just can't hold on to it and let that stuff fester. It'll just make you miserable."

"I guess." The misery I feel is covering my words.

"Sugar, Papa loves you."

"How are you so sure?"

"You're not?"

"I don't know what I am," I say.

Mrs. Pendleton cups my face with gentle hands and looks me in the eyes. "You are loved, sugar. You are loved with a depth you can't possibly fathom. I know you think your life should've been easier, but it wasn't. Not many people walk this earth who could go through what you've been through and have the gentle spirit you do. Even when you try to hide behind your hurt and pain, people see through it. They see the person you are. I know Uriah does."

"How can Papa love me and still put me through all this, though?"

"I don't have an answer. I'm not sure you will ever have an answer, but what I do know is that Papa does love you. Sometimes, we don't know His ways, but He knows us and we know Him, and that's what matters."

I take a slow, deep breath. "I wish I could understand."

"Well, maybe instead of understanding the situation, you just understand Papa. Understand He's been there and watched over you. He loves you, and His hands are all over your life. I can see it."

"Doesn't seem fair, though," I mutter.

"No, it doesn't. I can agree with you there."

"I don't want to stay mad at Papa. I know He's not the cause of all my woes, but it's hard when I know He's big and strong and I feel like He could have saved me from all of this."

Mrs. Pendleton nods. "I understand that, but we don't know what's down the street. What we think is bad is just Papa getting us ready for something we can't see. All those hurts, all those pains, all those worries and fears, are just lessons for things we can't see yet."

"What could it be?"

She smiles wide. "I don't know, but I have a feeling it's something truly amazing." She stands, helps me up, and pulls me into a hug. "Papa has big, big plans for you."

"I just wish I understood."

"I know. I wish I did too. I don't have all the answers for you. I don't know what Papa has planned or what the future will hold. I know that doesn't give you the answers you want, but sometimes all we have to hang our hope on is that Papa loves us."

I nod. "I know Papa loves me. I really do, but I wish sometimes I understood better."

"I know, sugar. I know. For now, we'll just hold on to the promise that He loves us and cling to His promise to work all things to our good."

Mrs. Pendleton's talk has helped me, but

I can't say I'm all that settled in my spirit about everything that's happened. I think part of what Papa wants from us is faith, and faith is a little harder than it sounds sometimes. The only thing I've got right now that's solid is that He loves me. For now, I'll hold tight to that.

CHAPTER THIRTY-SEVEN

A few weeks later, I go by Bo's office, after seeing Chrissy, to talk to him about my case and my daddy. Uriah wanted to come with me, but he had to go to work. He's started his own business, working on houses as a handyman.

Bo ushers me into his office, and I have a seat.

"You're looking good, Lilly. I see the cast is off."

"Yeah, I got it off a couple days ago. I

can't believe it's already been six weeks, but I can't say I miss it."

"No, doesn't feel like that much time has passed."

"Have you heard anything about my daddy?"

"Well, I told you a few weeks ago that Judge Kringle is holding him without bond. He's got a trial coming up soon, and we'll know then what's going to happen to him."

"You think he'll go to jail?"

Bo rubs his chin and gives me a confused look. "Honestly? I don't know. Judge Kringle usually surprises me. I hope he goes to jail. He needs to go to jail."

"Do you know who's representing him?"

Bo nods. "Yeah, he's a good lawyer. Someone out of Denton. I think he's related to a friend of your dad's."

I chew on my lip, nervous. "I pressed charges against him. I'm sure he knows it. If he gets out, Bo, he'll kill me. It's not a question. It's a fact."

"I know that. I just hope the judge thinks so," Bo says with a scowl. "If I hear anything, I'll let you know."

"What about my case?"

He smiles. "You're doing good. You've got about a month and a half of sessions left, and then Chrissy will give her report to the judge. He'll make his ruling from there. If things go like I think they will, you'll be free."

I nod. "I wish things could've been different."

"I know, but things have a way of happening the way they're supposed to happen." Bo smiles at me.

It's not as awkward as it was before, but I don't know if we'll ever be where we were. I won't say never because I've thought a lot of nevers lately that didn't seem to last as long as I thought never would.

I walk out of Bo's office and into the early September heat. The sun is beating down, and I decide I'll pay Fancy a visit. I haven't been in a long while, and I've missed talking to her.

When I get there, I open the door, and stale air hits me in the face. I'd almost forgotten how it smelled. Fancy's standing behind the bar and smiles when she sees me. Those glasses she's drying don't seem near as important because she drops them and races over to me, pulling me into a hug and fussing.

"I'm so glad to see you. I wanted to come visit you, but I didn't know if you'd want to see me or not 'cause of your daddy and all."

"I wish you had come to see me. I've missed you."

"Have a seat. I'll get us some drinks, and you can fill me in on what's been going on."

The seat in the corner is unoccupied.

I'm pretty sure my timing has a lot to do with it. One thing I notice is that Mr. Marlin isn't sitting at the bar. I've got my eyes fixed on what I suspect is his usual spot when Fancy returns with drinks.

She looks at me and then back at the bar. "Yeah, I told him he wasn't welcome no more."

"Why?"

"I didn't like his kind," she says with a wink.

"How did you know?"

"After the last time you were here, the look you two exchanged, somehow I just knew. So I told him his kind wasn't allowed in my bar no more." She lifts her nose a little. Her place might be a bar, but there are standards people have to meet.

"How'd he take it?"

She laughs. "With some cussin'."

I can't stop the grin from growing on my lips. "What did you do?"

With a snort, she inclines her head toward the bar. "I showed him the Browning I've got stowed behind the counter. Apparently, he speaks buckshot pretty well."

I look at Fancy, wide-eyed, and we bust out laughing. "I didn't know you had a shotgun behind there."

"Course I got a gun behind there. This here is a bar. People plus liquor can get mighty stupid."

"How you been, Fancy?"

"Oh, 'bout as good as a snapping turtle in a duck-filled pond. You doing okay?"

I look at my drink and play with the straw. "Oh, I guess. I'm only sore every once in a while now as opposed to constantly."

Fancy laughs. "Girl, you always were a funny one. You hear anything about George?"

"Just came from Bo's office. He said Daddy is being represented by a lawyer out of Denton. Bo says he's the relative of a friend or something. I don't care. I just hope he goes to jail."

"Well, just be prepared. He and Judge Kringle go way back. To tell the truth, I'm surprised he's in jail."

"I know. I've said the same thing. Uriah and his momma think I'm crazy. They think there's no way he'll get out, but they don't know him."

Fancy nods. "That man has connections. He knows people. I don't know who or how or why, but he does. If he gets out, sweetheart, I'm afraid the next time he comes for you, it won't be with his bare hands."

"No, next time he'll come with a gun, and he won't waste his energy. He'll just shoot me, and that'll be all she wrote."

"I'll never understand that man."

"He said he hated me. Said I reminded him of Will. Daddy said he hated Will, and my face reminded him of Will's."

Fancy looks at me solemnly and shakes her head. "Brush it off, sweetheart. That man's always been three fries short. I think all that moonshine he drank rotted his brain."

"I can try, but it sure doesn't feel good to know your daddy don't love you."

"You got other people who love you. Like that Uriah boy. He sure loves you." She states it like a fact.

"His momma does too." I hold Fancy's gaze. "Did you know she wanted me when I was little? I don't even remember going to her house or being around her."

"Oh yeah, your momma couldn't stand her because you loved on her. Oh my stars, you loved that woman. It was like the two of you was tied together from the moment you saw each other."

How much different could my life have been if I'd belonged to Mrs. Pendleton? I can't imagine it being any worse. "Then why didn't Momma just let her have me instead of being troubled with me?"

"'Cause your momma didn't think family should be with anyone but family. Lula loved you, Lilly. She just didn't love good."

I snort. "You don't have to tell me."

"Did Charlene tell you she wanted you?"

"Yeah, she told me. Shocked the tar out of me."

"Your momma did her best to keep the two of you apart, but when you'd go to church, you'd make a beeline. Now, that's what your momma would tell me. I wouldn't know. I've never stepped foot in that church. My folks have always gone the town over when we go to church."

I take a big sip of my drink. The soda feels good going down. The cold hits my stomach, and I can feel the fizzle all the way down. "Well, Fancy, I guess I need to get going."

We stand, and she bear-hugs me. "All right, sweetheart. Don't be a stranger, though, okay?"

I smile. "Yes, ma'am. I'll see you next week, okay?"

She waves as I walk out the door.

CHAPTER THIRTY-EIGHT

The next afternoon, Uriah and I are eating ice cream cones as we walk around the pond. We're walking and talking, and the clouds are drifting by, making the sun blink in and out, and I look at him and realize something I've probably known for a while now: I'm happy.

The feeling strikes me as funny because, for the longest time, I thought my lot in life was to be okay. Not mad or sad or anything, just okay. So, to feel happy is new for me.

I look at Uriah as he's walking next to me, and I also realize that had things not happened the way they did, I may not be standing here next to him. Now, that's not to say we wouldn't be together, but maybe it wouldn't be as good as the together we currently have.

I'm watching him trying to keep the ice cream from melting and running down his arm. He's wearing a pair of jeans and a t-shirt, and the breeze is blowing his hair, making it stand up in places. When he catches me looking at him, he smiles the same gorgeous smile I've come to find more endearing than heartbreaker.

"What are you gawking at? You've never seen a guy trying to keep an ice cream from melting before he can eat it?" Uriah asks, an eyebrow raised and his lips quirked up.

I can't help but giggle. "I love you, Uri-ah." It pops out before I can stop it.

Uriah stops dead in his tracks and looks

at me. His forgotten ice cream cone drips into the dirt. "What?"

For a moment, I stand there. I know I've said it. I know I mean it. I feel it in every inch of me. I swallow hard and repeat myself. "I love you, Uriah. I love you more than anything on this earth. I love you from the bottom of my heart. I've never loved anyone like I love you."

He pitches the cone to the side of the path and wraps his arms around me, pulling my head against his chest and resting his cheek on my hair. My ice cream slaps him on the back with a smack, and he lets out a small yelp.

"I'm getting ice cream on you," I say.

"I don't care." His mouth moves against my hair.

"I want my ice cream, Uriah."

He squeezes me tighter. "I'll buy you another on the way home."

With the promise of a new ice cream, I

pitch mine as far as I can throw it and hold on to him. "I'll keep you to that, ya know?"

"I don't care."

He holds me a long time like that. I'm not sure if it's because I said I love you or because he just wants to hold me. I don't care either way.

I still don't know how I feel about staying in Foaming Springs. I've got a lot of bad memories here. They're like ghosts jumping out at me everywhere I turn. Things and places reminding me of a bad home life.

Maybe if I stay, though, Uriah and I can create new memories that will wipe out the bad ones.

Uriah eventually lets me go and holds my hand, tangling his fingers in mine. Then he flashes a goofy smile, and I can't help but laugh.

"You owe me an ice cream."

"I know. I'll get you one on the way home. Right now, I want to walk the pond holding hands with the girl I love."

I can't meet his eyes. I'm somewhat embarrassed. I shouldn't be, but this is the first time I've ever told someone I love them. It's a funny feeling. A good feeling, but funny nonetheless.

We walk the pond a few times, and on the way home, Uriah stops for more ice cream. This time, we get some for his momma. I'm not sure how good of an idea it is, what with it being so hot, but we manage to get it to his momma with most of it still on the cone. The three of us sit on the porch, rocking, talking, and eating ice cream.

It's an interesting thing, I think as I sit with them, to be here. When I left Austin for Foaming Springs, my plan was to stay a few days and then go home. Now, there's a little bit of me that feels I am home. Uriah and his momma have made it feel like home.

After a while, Mrs. Pendleton goes into the house, leaving me and Uriah on the porch alone together. The breeze has picked up, and in true Texas form, a storm has started to brew. The clouds are dark, and lightning flashes in the distance as thunder rolls.

"I guess it's good we came home when we did," Uriah says.

"Guess so." The breeze picks up, and leaves that have accumulated on the porch swirl and dance. "I like this kind of weather. At the cabin, it was fun to watch all the trees."

Uriah gets real quiet. I can't read the expression on his face as he looks out over the yard. "Are you still leaving Foaming Springs when you're done with therapy?"

"I've been wondering about that myself.

I've got my business in Austin, and I've got you here."

"That doesn't really answer my question."

"That's because I don't know the answer. I've got so many bad memories here, like ghosts haunting me." I pause for a moment. Uriah watches me, anticipating disappointment. "I love you more than I hate those memories, though. I can't say it will be easy for me."

"How about this: I promise I will do all the grocery shopping for as long as you stay here. I promise to protect you from anyone who might do you harm. I promise to hold your hand when you're confused, hold you when you're scared, and love you for as long as I have breath."

I look at him, and he's smiling my favorite toothy grin. "I think that's fair, but what do you want in return?"

He takes my face in his hands and kisses my forehead. "You. I just want you."

I swallow hard. "Just me? I think you're getting the raw end of the deal."

As he keeps his eyes locked with mine, I see a sparkle in them I haven't seen before. "I don't think so."

Uriah's made sweet promises to me.

Papa, I'm going to make some promises, and you've got to help me keep them. Uriah may not have been through what I have been through, but his heart is just as tender as mine.

"I promise to tell you I love you when the weight of the world is on your shoulders. I promise to be the solid ground you can stand on when it seems like you're surrounded by quicksand. I promise to be there for you when you think the world is against you. I promise to hold your heart with care and love until I can no longer breathe."

Uriah stands, pulling me up with him and into a bear hug. "I love you, Lillian James," he says and kisses my forehead.

I love those kisses. I think they're my favorite kisses in the world. Those kisses say more than I love you. They give soft promises of hope and security.

My pulse jumps when I look in his eyes. I can see the love he feels for me, see it in his face, and it's better than pie, which is saying something for me. I've kissed men, but I've never kissed a man I love before.

I press my lips to his, and it shocks him. He quickly recovers and pulls me tighter to him, kissing me back.

The lightning booming in the sky hides the hammering of my heart as Uriah holds me and kisses me. It's like Papa is giving us a visual backdrop for how we feel about each other.

We stand on the porch, holding and

kissing each other until the rain starts blowing so hard we can't stand there anymore.

CHAPTER THIRTY-NINE

I'm looking out the window of Chrissy's office for the last time. It's the third week of October, but it's still as hot as it was in August. The sky is baby-blue, and the sun coming through the glass would be enough to melt me into the carpet if it weren't for the air conditioner.

My cast is off, but some of my bruises are healing slow. My ribs still ache from time to time. Daddy remains in jail waiting for his trial next month.

Chrissy and I have spent time talking

about what happened that day in the cabin, and she knows why I stabbed Daddy. He was going to hurt me, and I reacted. The reason I'd had trouble recalling it was, as Chrissy put it, my brain's way of dealing with the idea that he would hurt me.

"What was it like being at home with your dad when your mom would leave you there with him?" Chrissy asks.

As I stand there, I think hard. It's a crippling emotion as I begin to purposefully recall the times I spent with my daddy. "Well, you already know he was really sweet to me until I got to where I could talk good, somewhere between five and seven."

"Yes, I remember."

"He'd call me names. Say hateful things like I wish you were dead or I wish you'd just go for a walk and never come back. It's why I was in the woods that day."

Chrissy exhales sharply. "When you got lost?"

"Yeah. He told me to go and not come back. It's why she beat me. 'Cause I whispered that it was what Daddy told me to do."

"So she knew?"

"She knew. She just loved him more than me."

"Did he ever beat you or put his hands on you?"

"Sure. Just in places no one could see."

"Why didn't you tell anyone, Lilly?"

"Who woulda believed me? Remember? You knew him since you were little, and he was the nicest man ever?"

"But if you had marks?"

I turn to face Chrissy. The look on her face and the sympathy in her eyes make me bristle with anger. "It would've been my word against his, and if no one believed me, what do you think he would've done to me if I'd told and no one took me away from him? I wouldn't be standing here because he'd have killed me for sure."

"I understand. I just wish someone could've helped you."

I stroll to the chair facing Chrissy and sit. "Chrissy, most of this stuff I've buried so far down that it's hard to recall sometimes. Most of it feels like it's not real."

Chrissy nods. "It's your way of protecting yourself from hurtful memories."

I shake my head. "No, it's Papa's way of giving me peace. I can't change the past. I can't make it different."

"No, but I can understand if it makes you angry."

"I was. Am. Oh, I don't know. I'm frustrated more than anything. I should be able to just pick up and move on."

"Lilly, no one can do that."

"Why?"

"Because," Chrissy says, "you're allowed to feel angry, betrayed, hurt, let down, and frustrated. Not just allowed, but you have a right to feel them."

"I know I do. I think I'm just confused. I'm torn between wanting to be angry and wanting to do what Papa wants me to do."

"What does Papa want you to do?"

I fold my hands in my lap and look down at them. Papa and I have been having talks on the porch at night. I can feel the well of tears pooling in my eyes. "I hurt. I want Papa to let me be angry and mad. I want to be bitter. I want to hold on to what's happened to me, but Papa says doing that will make me feel worse. I don't know how I could possibly feel worse."

Chrissy simply nods her head.

"I want to be happy and forget all this ever happened, but at the same time, I feel like if I let it all go, I'm saying what happened was okay. That it makes it okay what Daddy did to me. I want those people that hurt me to get justice."

"But what does Papa say?" Chrissy asks.

I look at Chrissy and chew on the inside of my cheek. "Papa says I need to forgive them. That I need to let go of the hurt and anger. It's the only way to be truly free."

"You did that with Bo."

"Bo didn't nearly beat me to death."

Chrissy shakes her head. "No, he didn't."

"Daddy hurt me more than one time and deeply." The ugly cry that's been sitting at the edge comes spilling over, and I can't stop it from pouring out.

Chrissy jumps out of the chair and envelops me in a hug quicker than a wink. "It's okay, Lilly," she says softly.

I don't know how long I cry, but she never lets me go until I'm done. Between talking to Papa, Mrs. Pendleton, Uriah, and now Chrissy, the past few weeks have helped, but it's also thrown a light on my past that I wanted to keep hidden, creating an emotional volcano, building and building until I can't hold it in anymore.

When I stop crying, Chrissy holds me by the shoulders. "That's been a long time coming, huh?"

"I guess so. All this talk of the past."

Her hands grip my shoulders tighter, and she keeps her gaze locked on me. "You know, not talking about things, hiding them? It only makes it worse. It makes you feel like you deserved it, but you don't. You didn't deserve any of it."

"I guess."

"No," Chrissy says sternly. "No. No guess. You didn't."

"Bad things happen to everyone, Chrissy."

"That doesn't mean it's right. It just means it happens."

I nod quietly.

Her lips purse, and then she leans in a little. "You listen to me, Lillian James. None of this stuff was your fault. None of this had anything to do with you. You were a child. I don't know how I would've handled it."

"Same as me. You just would have."

Chrissy shakes her head. "I don't think so."

"You never know. I hope you never do. I wouldn't wish it on anyone."

Her eyes water. "No, I wouldn't either. Knowing what I know now, you are perhaps the strongest person I've ever met. I don't know if I could've made the choices you have."

I shrug. "I didn't see any choices."

"That's what makes you strong. Where others would've seen choices, you saw one path."

"That doesn't make me strong. I just did what Papa told me to do."

"Not everyone would've done that."

"I don't know about that."

Chrissy stands and pulls me into another hug. "I do."

She lets me go, and I look at the clock. "It's way past my hour."

"It's all right, Lilly."

I look down at the floor. It embarrasses me to let my emotions get the better of me.

Chrissy must feel it, because when I look at her again, she's smiling.

"I guess I should get going. Uriah's probably outside, wondering if everything's okay."

"I'll see ya next week?"

"Do I have a choice?"

Chrissy's shoulders bounce as she laughs. "Yes, but I hope you will. We're friends, right?"

"Yeah, I'll see you next week."

CHAPTER FORTY

Uriah and I go to dinner two towns over as a celebration of my release from therapy. A few days ago, I finished my required number of sessions. During court, Bo and Chrissy both vouched for me, and since my daddy nearly killed me, Judge Kringle seemed to think my actions were, albeit rash, justified in light of what happened.

Talking with Chrissy was good for me. I learned about myself, got things off my chest, and Chrissy and I ended therapy as good friends. I have a real friend. The notion still boggles me.

The steakhouse Uriah and I are in is super nice. I've got my best dress on, and he's wearing nice slacks and a polo shirt. He's so handsome, looking better now than he did in high school.

I check out the menu. Everything looks good. I find a meal that calls to me: a small steak, baked sweet potato fries, and baked apples. My mouth waters just reading it.

Our waiter takes our order and leaves. Uriah is looking at me with a goofy grin. "You okay, Uriah?"

"I'm fine."

"You sure. You're lookin' kinda—"

He pops up from the chair and gets down on one knee.

My eyes bug out. I know exactly what's happening, and it throws me for a loop.

Uriah pulls a little velvet box from his

pocket and looks up at me, those green eyes sparkling. It makes me melt.

"Lillian James," he says and opens the box. A beautiful little ring sits nestled in it. "I have loved you since the first time I saw you. I love your spirit, I love your ways, I love the way you love Papa, and, most of all, I love you. Will you do me the honor of becoming my wife?"

I put my hand to my mouth, too shocked to speak. Uriah is looking at me with those big green eyes full of love and hope.

"Yes," I say. It pops out without any thought whatsoever. He's trusting me with his heart as much as I'm trusting him with mine.

Uriah slips the ring on my finger and grabs me up out of the chair, swinging me around.

I'm holding on for dear life, thinking, *Thank you, Papa.*

For a list of all books by Bree Livingston, please visit her website at www.breelivingston.com.

ABOUT THE AUTHOR

Bree Livingston lives in the West Texas Panhandle with her husband, children, and cats. She'd have a dog, but they took a vote and the cats won. Not in numbers, but attitude. They wouldn't even debate. They just leveled their little beady eyes at her and that was all it took for her to nix getting a dog. Her hobbies include...nothing because she writes all the time.

She loves carbs, but the love ends there. No, that's not true. The love usually winds up on her hips which is why she loves writing romance. The love in the pages of her books are sweet and clean, and they definitely don't add pounds when you step on the scale. Unless of course, you're actually holding a Kindle while you're weighing. Put the Kindle down and try again. Also, the cookie because that could be the problem too. She knows from experience.

Join her mailing list to be the first to find out publishing news, contests, and more by going to her website at https://www.breelivingston.com.

- facebook.com/BreeLivingstonWrites
- twitter.com/BreeLivWrites
- instagram.com/breelivwrites
- bookbub.com/authors/bree-livingston
- amazon.com/author/breelivingston

Manufactured by Amazon.ca
Bolton, ON